	DATE DUE		MAR 2 3 2009
orange	Blue	NOV 12	
NOV 27 '87	APR 23 '90	JAN 2 1 1999	MAY 2 4 2007
NOV 27 '87 of	Yellow	FEB -4 1999	MAR 2 3 2008
Purple	OCT 24 '90	FEB 2 6 1999	MAR 2 3 2008
MAR 18 '88	red	MAR 1 1 1999	MAR 2 3 2009
red	JUN 29 '91	APR 1 5 1999	
JAN 23 '90	purple	MAY 1 0 1999	MAR 2 3 2009
Blue	JUN 4 '92	NOV 30	SEP 2 3 2009
FEB 9 '90	Yellow	DEC	MAR 2 3 2009
purple	NOV 11 '93	SEP 2 6 2002	MAR 2 3 2009
MAR 23 '90	DEC 4 '94	APR 1 8 2003	MAR 2 3 2009

BOOKS BY BARBARA CORCORAN

A
HORSE
NAMED
SKY

BARBARA CORCORAN

A HORSE NAMED SKY

ATHENEUM   1986   NEW YORK

Library of Congress Cataloging-in-Publication Data

Corcoran, Barbara.   A horse named Sky.

SUMMARY: Georgia's one goal, when she and her mother
move to Montana to get away from her alcoholic father,
is to own a horse, a dream that seems remote until
her next door neighbor promises to sell her a wild mustang.
[1. Horses—Fiction.   2. Family problems—Fiction.
3. Montana—Fiction] I. Title.
PZ7.C814Ho 1986   [Fic]   85-20060
ISBN 0-689-31193-1

TO
Lisa Rogers

My thanks to

LINDA WALCH & JEANNE DIXON

for information on
the idiosyncracies of horses.

A
HORSE
NAMED
SKY

1

SOMETHING TERRIBLE HAS HAPPENED!
Georgia wrote the words carefully in capital letters
on the first page of the journal that she had bought
with Aunt Maisie's birthday money. It was a big journal, and there were many blank pages waiting to be
written on. A life waiting to be lived.

But what a sad beginning. She read what she had
written and resisted the impulse to hunch over as if
someone might be looking over her shoulder. But
there was no one to look. Her mother was at work at
the Chamber of Commerce, her sister Marge was two
states away at college. Her father . . . She didn't know
where he was. He would ordinarily have been at
work, but he had lost his job. Again. That was the
fourth job in two years he had lost, not because he
wasn't very good as a bank manager, but because he

thought he was so good, he could tell his boss how to run things. It always ended, as it had yesterday, with his losing his temper and yelling at the boss and getting fired. Four times in two years. That was bad.

But it wasn't the worst thing. That was what had happened last night, downstairs in the kitchen. Half closing her eyes, she wrote again in capitals: HE BEAT UP MY MOTHER. Then she closed the diary quickly. The words were too painful to look at. She wished she had written in pencil, so she could erase them.

But she couldn't stop remembering. She had been in her room doing homework when she heard the fight start. At dinner, when he had announced that he had resigned from the branch bank where he worked, her mother had turned white, but she had been very controlled. She even seemed almost sympathetic while he raved on about how stupid his boss was, how he didn't recognize talent when he saw it. Maybe he really had quit; there was never any way to know whether he resigned or was fired, but the end result was the same. It meant Mom would have to deal with the expenses while he looked for another job. And with his recent record, a job wouldn't be all that easy to find.

She had been trying not to think about it, to concentrate on her algebra, but she had heard their voices rising. Then she heard a crash and she ran downstairs. Her mother was leaning against the counter, bent over with her hand to her face. Georgia had realized in a sickening flash that he had been hitting her. She flew at him and bit his hand.

He raised his hand to hit her, and she heard her mother cry out. He didn't hit her though. Instead, he stared down at her for a second, then stormed out of the house, and they heard his car take off.

"He's gone to his mother's," Georgia's mother said.

Georgia helped her upstairs and got her to bed. She wanted to call the doctor and the police, but her mother said no. And Georgia knew why. The last time he had yelled and threatened, her mother had called the police, but they said they couldn't do anything about a family squabble. A family squabble. Did you have to get killed before they would help?

She put the diary away hastily as she heard a car come into the yard. It would be her mother. Georgia's cat jumped into her lap, and she shifted him to her shoulder. "We'd better see if Mom's okay."

Her mother was in the kitchen. She smiled at Georgia, but she looked awful. Her left eye was puffed and discolored, and there was a bruise beside her mouth.

"Mom, are you all right?" It was a dumb question.

"Sure, honey." Her mother sat down. "I've got news for you." She looked at Georgia with a mixture of anxiety and hope. "Please be glad."

"What is it?" Georgia was almost afraid to hear.

[5]

"We're going to leave. Really, at last. After all the times I've threatened to, we're going to do it." Her mother took a deep breath. "How does that strike you?"

"Where are we going?" She tried to think what it would be like to live in another house. Another town.

"To another state. Another place altogether. I've had it, Georgia. I've had it." She looked as if she might cry.

Georgia sat down across from her. "Where are we moving to?"

"Lolo, Montana."

"What?" In spite of her distress, Georgia almost laughed. It sounded so funny.

"Lolo, Montana, in the Bitter Root Valley of the Treasure State, Big Sky Country. How does that grab you?"

Georgia couldn't figure out what she felt. There was a rising surge of excitement, a feeling of escape near at hand, yet a nostalgia for the old life that she hadn't yet left. "It grabs me good. I think. I mean, it sounds weird . . ." She giggled.

Her mother reached across the table and caught her hands. "Oh, honey, I hope it's going to work. It's got to work. I've put up with everything too long. So have you. We owe ourselves a decent life. Don't we?"

"Sure," Georgia said. "Sure we do. Have they got schools?"

Now it was her mother's turn to laugh. "You

bet. They've got schools, and cowboys and Indians, and buffalo and deer and horses . . ."

"Horses?" Georgia perked up. "Can I have a horse?"

"I don't even have a job yet, but somehow or other we'll get you a horse. It won't be an Arabian or a quarterhorse or anything elegant, but it'll be a four-footed beast with a saddle on him. I promise."

Georgia forgot everything else, at least for the moment. "Oh, wow," she said softly. "I'm going to name him . . ." She thought for a minute. ". . . Sky. For Big Sky."

2

THE NIGHT was inky black when they left, with
no moon, no stars. It was a little after midnight as her
mother backed the van out of the garage. It was loaded
with the things they had packed in a hurry. Georgia
was trying not to think about all the things she had to
leave behind: some of her clothes, a lot of her books,
records. She took her new stereo though, and the
small radio-cassette player, and all her tapes. If she had
had time, she would have transferred the best of the
records onto tape.

Her father had not come back or called. He
would be at Grandmother's. He always went there
when he had problems. Grandmother was a retired
opera singer, and she was rich. She thought her son
had married beneath him. Furthermore, Marge was
her favorite, not Georgia. Definitely not Georgia.

Georgia's mother didn't turn on the car lights

until they were out of the driveway and halfway down the block. "Like thieves in the night," she muttered. No one knew they were leaving except Aunt Maisie and Jill at the Chamber of Commerce. It was Jill who had friends in Lolo, Montana, and had called and arranged for Georgia and her mother to rent a small furnished house from them. Jill had also come by and picked up Georgia's cat.

Georgia hated not being able to say goodbye, especially to her best friend Connie. And her English teacher, Miss Cassidy. The school year had only begun, but already Georgia knew she loved Miss Cassidy. She wondered what everyone would say when they found out she was gone. It gave her a sinking feeling to think of all of them going on in the usual way, and she wouldn't be there.

The streetlights looked dim. The lights in Jerry Baker's house were still on. It was hard to leave town just when Jerry was beginning to notice her.

She scrunched down in her seat, struck with the crazy idea that Jerry could see her running away. Because that was what they were doing, running away. Running a long, long way, too far for her father to come after them. Maybe he wouldn't even want to.

She tried to concentrate on her horse. Sky. She had been thinking about him ever since her mother said they were going. In her mind she saw a sleek Arabian, although she knew they couldn't afford anything like that. A good Arabian cost thousands of dollars. But maybe Sky would be the runt of the litter or the wrong color or something so she could get him cheap. It wouldn't spoil him. He would be fast and graceful and beautiful, and he would love her as much as she loved him. She hoped he would be a colt, and she could train him herself. Not that she had ever trained a horse, but she could learn. Sky would make up for everything bad that had happened.

The motion of the car made her sleepy. She curled up, one leg tucked under her. She hoped there would be a music teacher in Lolo, Montana. Next to horses, her greatest love was music. Mrs. Endicott would wonder what had happened to her. She put her arm behind her to check that her cassettes were there. She was glad she had taped all those old opera records of her father's.

For a minute she thought about him as he had been when she was younger, before his temper began to get out of hand. Their big bond had been music. He took her sometimes to the opera, when it came to Boston, and to concerts. He paid for her music lessons. He had seemed almost proud of her back then. But that was too painful to think about.

She reached out and turned on the car radio. A late disc jockey was playing old-time musical comedy records. Georgia fell asleep listening to "I've Got You Under My Skin."

IT WAS DAWN when she woke. Her mother said, "You're just in time for the tag-end of the Mohawk

Trail. Too bad we had to do it in the dark. The scenery is pretty."

Georgia stretched and yawned. "Is it time for breakfast?"

"Soon."

When they faced each other across a booth in a small all-night restaurant, Georgia was shocked to see how tired her mother looked. She wished she could drive, to help out. She knew how, but she was only thirteen.

She had thought she was too unhappy to eat, but she found herself enjoying two eggs over easy, hash browns, toast and marmalade, and milk.

Her mother ate silently, looking up now and then to give Georgia a wan smile.

"What if he tells the cops to look for us?"

She sipped her coffee. "The van's in my name. There's nothing he can do."

Georgia had the feeling that her mother was saying that to herself for reassurance. If he got mad enough, there was a lot he could do, she was sure. If he cared enough.

"What if he tries to get Aunt Maisie to tell him where we've gone?"

Her mother gave her a thin smile. "Maisie and Jack leave for Bermuda this afternoon."

"That's right. I forgot." She felt somewhat relieved. She was very fond of her Aunt Maisie. She didn't want her father hassling her. By the time she and Uncle Jack got home from their Bermuda vacation, maybe he would have cooled down. Maybe.

"Let's go," her mother said. "You're finished, aren't you?"

Georgia nodded. She was anxious to be gone, too. "I'd like my horse to be a colt," she said, as her mother shifted into high.

"What?"

"My horse. I want to train him myself."

"Oh," her mother said absently. "Right."

They drove all day, stopping finally, exhausted and hot, at a small, inexpensive motel on the edge of a town in New York State.

While her mother was in the shower, Georgia got out her journal. At the top of the second page she wrote: ON OUR WAY. She wanted to write down something about the day's journey, a kind of travelogue. But all she could think about was home. Cinders, the calico cat, who was now with Jill. Had they told Jill that Cinders liked Kal-Kan Dinner for Finicky Eaters? That was the one he would always eat, when he turned up his nose at other things. And what was Miss Cassidy thinking, when she wasn't there to turn in her theme on Puccini? Was there any point in mailing it to her? Maybe it would be useful in Lolo, Montana. They probably asked for themes there, too.

She thought about Jerry. He'd be in bed early, because he took training seriously. It was his first year on the team. She wrote in the journal: "Good luck, Jerry."

Tomorrow she would write a long letter to Connie, not to tell her where they were going, just to say hello and good-by.

She closed the journal, finally, too tired to write any more. As she stretched her long legs down the length of the narrow bed, suddenly tears came. She buried her face in her pillow so her mother wouldn't see.

3

AT NIAGARA FALLS they went over into Canada. Georgia made a note in her journal: FIRST FOREIGN COUNTRY. There was a lot of forest, and although the countryside seemed to stretch ahead endlessly, the other cars on the road drove as if possessed, overtaking each other, cutting in, speeding. "Like big city drivers," her mother said. Otherwise Georgia could see no difference in Canadians except that they said "oot" and "aboot" for "out" and "about," and they tacked an "eh?" onto the ends of sentences. She wrote it all down.

Driving through northern Michigan, the pace was slower, but the heavy stands of forest depressed her. She felt like Gretel in "Hansel and Gretel," and she wondered if she would ever be able to find her way home again. Hoping to make her mother smile, she said, "We ought to be leaving a trail of crumbs."

But her mother stared ahead at the ribbon of road and said, "It's all right with me if I never find my way back."

That shook Georgia. Till now she had thought of this as a trip. They would go away for a while, and her father would miss them, and he'd straighten out and get his old disposition back, and everything would be fine. But if her mother was thinking of it as forever . . .

The miles went by; and she began to feel as if she were in a dream. Michigan, Wisconsin, Minnesota, North Dakota . . . She was losing her power to observe. More and more, she played tapes, one after the other, mostly opera but some pop tunes and some rock. Finally her mother begged for an interval of silence.

"Just for fifteen minutes or so, honey. My head is spinning."

"You don't really like music, do you." She said it because she was tired and unhappy. Her mother always said she had a tin ear, but she was a bit defensive about it; Georgia knew she didn't like to be reminded. Before her mother could answer, she said, "I won't play them for a while. My head's kind of ringing, too."

She closed her eyes and slept a while. It was her mother's voice, sounding excited for the first time, that woke her.

"Look!" she was saying. "Georgia, look."

"What? What is it?"

"Look around you. We're out west."

It *was* different. The earth seemed to have opened

up in endless vistas. She could look in all directions as far as the horizon, without trees to block her view. The sky, bright blue and cloudless, came down around them like a vast bowl turned upside down. She took a long breath.

"Is this Montana?"

"No, it's North Dakota, but isn't it great? Don't you feel free?"

Georgia shaded her eyes. "Looks like you could fall off the edge."

Her mother laughed. It was the first time Georgia had heard her laugh since they left home. "That's what they told Columbus." She reached over and squeezed Georgia's hand. "I think we've got ourselves a New World."

I hope so, Georgia thought, I hope so. It looked awfully big. But then she saw some horses racing across the plain, and she felt better. Maybe it was going to be okay after all.

4

SHE THOUGHT they would never come to the end of North Dakota. It really must have been country like this where people thought you could come to the edge of the world and fall off.

She got into the back seat and listened to Maria Callas tapes, thinking about how terrible it would be to have a voice like that and to lose it. It would be worse than having to run away from your father.

But she was not going to feel sorry for herself. Kids moved all the time. In her own school at least five kids she knew had moved away in the last two years. Fathers got transfered. She sighed. Hers would never hold on to a job long enough to get transfered.

She pulled up the collar of her sweater. North Dakota was chilly. In this case, it was the mother who got transfered. Moms had just as much right as dads had to move. Only Mom didn't even have a job.

She'll get one. Georgia closed her eyes. Mom was a real good coper. Don't worry, don't worry. She dozed and then jerked awake, thinking for a second that her cat was curled up in her lap; but when she reached for him, there was nothing there.

"Mom, are you sure you told Jill about Cinders liking Finicky Eaters?"

"I told her, dear. I wrote out a whole list of instructions." Her eyes met Georgia's in the mirror. "Don't worry. Jill loves cats." She pointed to the fields ahead of them. "We're in Montana."

Georgia sat up abruptly. "Honestly? Why didn't you tell me?"

"You were asleep."

Georgia studied the landscape. "It looks just like North Dakota."

"It will change when we get to the mountains."

"What mountains?"

Her mother laughed. "You never were brilliant at geography, were you, honey. The Rockies." There was a new note in her voice. A happier note. A tinge of excitement. She had always liked to travel, but Georgia's father hated it, so they almost never went anywhere. Georgia wondered which she was: traveler or stay-at-home. She was sure going to find out, in spite of herself.

THAT NIGHT, in a big motel room with bright pink walls and odd but interesting abstract art, they called Georgia's sister Marge. Her mother had called her the first night of the trip, but this was the first time Georgia had talked to her.

Marge still sounded amazed that they had just taken off. Her father had called her the night before to see if she knew where they were, but she could truthfully say she didn't know. Now her mother told her.

"Montana!" Marge said, when Georgia came on the line. "You might as well have gone to Katmandu."

Georgia was feeling the same way, and it irritated her to have Marge echo her concern. Defensively she said, "It's terrific. You can see for miles."

"What can you see?"

Marge always asked unanswerable questions. Georgia changed the subject. "How are your classes?"

"Super. I've switched my major."

"Again! How many times is that now?"

"Oh, everybody does it. I switched to drama. Put Mom back on so I can tell her. And Georgie, have a good time. I mean try to get a lot out of it. It's an experience."

"I'm going to get a horse."

"Great. Let me talk to Mom."

Georgia gave her mother the phone and went out to sit in the dim light by the empty pool. She and Marge had never been close. There was a seven-year gap between them. She would not especially miss Marge. And Marge wouldn't miss them. She had left them all behind when she went to college two years ago. Anyway she was Daddy's favorite, so they could console each other if anybody needed consoling.

"Experience." She wasn't sure she longed for experience at this point in time. She wanted to have her cat and talk to Jerry between classes and have her music lessons and spend the night at Connie's, eating pizza and drinking root beer. Tears filled her eyes.

I'm going to have a horse named Sky, she reminded herself. Beautiful, fast. We'll ride like the wind. And maybe race at the county fair.

5

GEORGIA'S MOTHER was reading two books at once. Not really quite at once, but she read one for an hour or so and then took up the other one. The books were *The Bloody Bozeman* by Dorothy M. Johnson, and *The Way West*, by A. B. Guthrie, Jr. She was exclaiming with delight over both of them, stopping every now and then to read a passage aloud to Georgia.

Georgia did not want to hear about the way west or the bloody Bozeman. All day she had endured the way west and the bloody Bozeman trail. She didn't want even to think about them. While her mother had carried on with enthusiasm about the beauty of the mountain passes they were going through, Georgia had squinched her eyes tight shut, trying not to picture the chasms that fell away on their left and trying not to imagine that the jagged cliffs that towered above them on their right were falling in on them.

Finally her mother had said, "Sweetie, do you suppose you have acrophobia?"

"Probably," Georgia said between clenched teeth, not knowing what the word meant.

"A fear of heights? I've never noticed. Are you nervous about being high up in buildings?"

"I haven't been high up in any buildings." Georgia opened one eye, saw a red cliff close enough to touch, and shut her eye again.

By the time they got to the motel on the northern outskirts of Bozeman, Georgia felt as if she had aged twenty years.

"Lolo is in a valley," her mother said, looking over at her. "There's Ravalli Valley, and right next to it is Missoula Valley. There'll be mountains, but they won't be as close to us as they were today."

"Thank the Lord for small favors," Georgia muttered, repeating a favorite expression of Aunt Maisie's.

"You'll like it, Georgia. Just give it a chance. I know it's a culture shock, but it's going to be a really enriching experience for both of us."

Experience again. What if she didn't feel like having experiences? Could you shut them off for a while?

THAT NIGHT she dreamed she was the filling in a mountain sandwich. She woke up gasping for breath. Her mother was sleeping quietly. Moonlight filtered through a crack in the heavy drapes. Georgia got up and looked out the window. The mountains, at a little distance now, looked ghostly in the moonlight. Like mist. Like the mountains you see sometimes in Japanese prints, as if they floated with no connection to earth. She thought of Madame Butterfly. Pain came to people in all kinds of situations. Well, she would never deal with it by killing herself. For one thing, you might miss something wonderful. If she died right this minute, she wouldn't get to hear the new season of Met broadcasts, for instance. She wouldn't get her horse. She'd never be any better at singing than she was now. Maybe she wouldn't be better anyway, but at least she could try.

She shivered and got back into bed. Maybe her mother wouldn't mind if she wrote Jill a postcard and reminded her about Finicky Eaters for Cinders.

6

GEORGIA GOT OFF the school bus and walked into the back yard. "My yard. And that tiny house with peeling blue paint is where I live. Georgia Blake, Lolo, Montana. Eighth grade, Big Rock School." It sounded like a foreign language, but she repeated it every day, trying to make it real.

She had goofed again today at school. She'd gone barreling into the boys' gym instead of the girls'. The teacher had been nice about steering her out, but she could hear the boys' guffaws. Yesterday some kid had suggested a turkey shoot in November to raise money for the girls' basketball team, and she had said, "Oh, no! There must be a better way to raise money than shooting turkeys." They had all screamed with laughter, because it turned out that a turkey shoot was where the person who was the best shot won a turkey. How was she supposed to know? She'd grown up in a small suburban community in Massachusetts where nobody shot anything, except sometimes each other. That had been one of her nightmares, that her father would get a gun.

The van was gone. Her mother was job-hunting again. She had gone out every day since they came, looking for a job. Jill's friends, their landlords, had made some suggestions, but nothing had come of it. So her mother came home every night, worn out and discouraged and more and more panicky. What if there weren't any jobs? What if they had to give up and go home? Georgia couldn't sort out how she felt about that. They couldn't go back to things as they had been, but she longed for the familiar, secure surroundings and the friends that she had left.

She went into the house and made a peanut butter sandwich and poured a glass of milk. Just the way she would have done at home. Only this kitchen was tiny, like a doll house, and the peanut butter wasn't the same kind, and there was no cat to jump into her arms, no Connie to giggle with. Mrs. Salton was an okay teacher, but she wasn't Miss Cassidy, and none of the boys looked like Jerry. She ached with homesickness.

She hadn't mentioned the horse. Her mother was too worried about making her savings last. When the money was gone, it was gone. And she swore she wouldn't take any help from Georgia's father. Not that he was likely to offer it, or had it to offer.

Georgia had noticed a farm down the road with horses. The Ross place. Her mother had gotten acquainted with old Mrs. Ross, who owned the place. There were several horses in the pasture. If she could get a horse, somehow, that would make all the difference.

She decided to walk down the road toward the Ross farm. Maybe she could just say hello and get a look at the horses. Maybe they had one they would sell cheap. She wished she could get a job herself after school.

Old Mrs. Ross was out in the yard tossing corn to some scraggly-looking chickens. She moved stiffly from arthritis, but she stood straight. As Georgia came within hearing, she realized that Mrs. Ross was giving the hens a piece of her mind.

The barn, a lot bigger than the house, stood at some distance behind it. Beyond the barn and to the left there was a field where Mrs. Ross's grandson, a seventeen-year-old boy named Marty, was working with a horse. He had the horse on a long rope, and he stood in the middle of the field, letting the horse go around and around in a wide circle. Georgia had noticed Marty Ross before. He was handsome, in a rugged way, but to her he was an adult. She liked to look at good-looking older men the way she liked to look at a Tom Selleck poster, but if they spoke to her, she was likely to get tongue-tied.

Her mother had told her that Marty's mother was dead, and his father, Elmore Ross, worked for a company that built log cabins. Georgia had seen Elmore driving by in an old pickup.

" 'Day to you," Mrs. Ross said, turning around with her whole body, as if she couldn't move her head separately.

"Hello," Georgia said. And then because something else seemed to be called for, she added, "Nice day."

"Beauty," Mrs. Ross said. She flung the last of the corn at the hens. "Come and set, if you've a mind to." She marched to the back steps and stiffly settled herself on the top step. Georgia sat down on a lower step.

Mrs. Ross said, "Where you come from, this time of year's red. Out here it's gold." She gestured toward the distant mountains.

"That's right, it is." Georgia was surprised that she hadn't noticed that.

"It's all those western larch up on the mountains. Some call it tamarack, but western larch is what it is. You remember that."

"All right," Georgia said. "I will."

"Folks ought to name things right."

Georgia leaned back a little so she could look at the wrinkled, angular face with the firm jaw and the vivid blue eyes. Mrs. Ross looked a thousand years old except for the eyes. "I guess you must have been back East?"

"Grew up in Rhode Island."

"Really?" Georgia was amazed.

Mrs. Ross laughed, a short dry laugh almost like a cough. "You young 'uns figure if somebody's in one place, specially someone as old as me, they must have been there forever."

"Yes, I guess I do," Georgia said. "Maybe someday someone will be surprised when I say I'm from Massachusetts."

They were silent for a few minutes, Mrs. Ross staring off into space, Georgia thinking about the strangeness of being where she was.

"You like cats?" Mrs. Ross broke the silence.

"Oh, yes. I had to leave my cat at home."

"You think your mama'll let you have a kitten?"

Georgia sat up straight. "Oh, I know she would. She likes cats, too."

"Old Tabby had her another batch. You go down to the barn and look 'em over. Pick one out."

Georgia jumped up, feeling happier than she had since she had left home. "Thank you very, very much. That's wonderful."

"They're in the first horse stall. Give me a hand up." She held out her hand, crooked from arthritis, and Georgia helped her to her feet. "Terrible nuisance to get stuck with arthritis at my age." She gave Georgia a piercing glance. "I'm only seventy-nine."

"That's not old at all," Georgia said politely.

"Ha!" Mrs. Ross turned to her back door, reaching for it for support before she took the last step. "It's older than Methuselah, and he was as old as the mountains. Git along now and pick out your kitten." She went inside, letting the screen door slam.

Georgia ran to the barn. It was dim and cool inside, and for a moment she couldn't see anything. Then as her eyes adjusted to the light, she saw that three of the stalls had horses in them, all three of them peering at her inquisitively. She stopped to pat each one. The bay mare jerked away from her nervously, but the other two, a chestnut and a gray, stood patiently, looking at her with big, dark eyes.

After a few minutes she remembered the kittens. She found them with their mother in a far corner of an empty stall. They were old enough to be playful, and as she came into the stall, they rushed up to her and fell over her ankles in a heap. One was pure white with very blue eyes, and the other two were gray with faint dark stripes. The mother was silvery gray. She watched quietly as Georgia scooched down and petted the kittens.

"Your children are beautiful," Georgia told the mother cat. "How can I choose?" She sat on the straw and took the kittens into her lap.

She forgot about time. First one kitten, then another, seemed to her the one she wanted most. She jumped when she suddenly heard the heavy, clomping feet of a horse coming into the barn. A man's voice said, "Whoo, girl, easy."

The horse and Marty Ross loomed in the faint light of the barn. He didn't glance toward the empty stall. Georgia didn't know whether to speak or not. She was scared. He might think she was an intruder.

But if she didn't speak up, and then he saw her, that would be worse. She put the kittens down, got to her feet, and said, "Hello," in a faint voice.

He didn't hear her. The horse was stomping and whinnying, and Marty was talking to her. "Whoa there, old girl, hold still, you witch. Get in there, go on, git."

Georgia stepped to the entrance of the stall and spoke louder, in a voice that cracked. "Uh . . . hello. Mr. Ross?"

He whirled around, startled. "Holy smoke!" he said. "You want to scare somebody to death?"

"I'm sorry . . ."

"Who are you?"

"I'm . . . I live down the road. I'm Georgia Blake."

"Oh," he said. "Hi." He turned away to attend to the horse.

"Your grandmother said I could have a kitten."

"Good," he said over his shoulder. "Take 'em all."

"All?" Did he mean it? She looked down at the three kittens, tumbling over each other. "Would your grandmother mind?"

"Mind?" He laughed. "She'd be tickled pink. There'll be a new batch before you know it. We got the busiest cat in the valley."

"You've got nice horses."

"They're boarders."

"Oh." Georgia felt disappointed. She had half

thought maybe she could get him to sell her one, when her mother had the money.

She started to ask him again if it really was okay to take all the kittens, but then in her mind she heard her father saying impatiently, "Georgia, why do you ask the same thing over and over? If I've told you once, I've told you a hundred times . . ." She gathered up the kittens in her arms. "I hope you won't be lonesome," she said softly to the mother cat.

Marty Ross laughed. He had closed the half-door of the stall and was standing behind her. "She'll survive."

"Are they old enough to leave her?"

"Yep. They're weaned."

"I'll take good care of them."

"What'll your mom say?"

Georgia hadn't thought about it. Her mother liked cats, but she might be a bit startled at getting three. "Oh, she won't mind," she said, hoping she sounded convincing. "We're cat people."

"Yeah?" He looked amused. "Me, I'm a horse person." He ran his hand along the velvety nose of the bay mare who had turned away from Georgia.

"Do the owners come here to ride them?"

"Yep. If they was mine, they'd be up on the mountain."

Georgia had seen horses grazing partway up a mountain and had wondered. "They don't stay there all winter, do they?"

" 'Course they do. Where you from?"

"Massachusetts."

"Thought so. A dude, like my grandma."

"She doesn't seem like a dude." She shifted the kittens to keep them from falling. One of them chewed on her wrist.

"She comes from back East. Once a dude, always a dude. See ya." He gave her a wave and strode off toward the house.

Georgia hesitated when she came to the back porch. Should she ask Mrs. Ross if it was all right to take all the kittens? She didn't see her anywhere around. Maybe she was taking a nap. The old ladies Georgia knew took naps. She decided to leave well enough alone.

The van was in the barn when Georgia got home. She took a deep breath and marched into the house. "Mom?" she began calling, as soon as she was inside. "Mom? Guess what we've got!"

Her mother came into the kitchen and looked at her. "Oh, dear heaven! That's all we need. Kittens! How many? It looks like a dozen . . ."

"It's only three, Mom." Georgia talked fast, before her mother could interrupt. "Mrs. Ross gave them to me. At least she said take one, and her grandson said take them all. They're awfully cute. And there's only three of them."

Her mother sighed. "Already named, I suppose. Already settled in."

"I'm going to name them Ping, Pang, and Pong."

In spite of herself her mother laughed. "Something to do with Ping-Pong?"

"No, after the three characters in *Turandot*, the Chinese characters. Ping is the grand Chancellor, Pang, is the Purveyor, and Pong is the Chief Cook."

"I'll never know which is which."

"It won't matter, you see, because the names are so much alike, they'll answer to all three."

Her mother shook her head. "Thank God it's not three horses."

"Did you find a job, Mom?"

"No. I did not find a job."

And that, Georgia knew, meant don't ask about a horse. Not yet.

7

THE NEXT DAY after school, four children went by Georgia's house. She recognized the horses. They were the ones she had seen at the Rosses': a bay, an Appaloosa, a gray, and a big black one. She watched them. These kids must be the owners.

The oldest was a girl about sixteen who slumped in her saddle as if she lived there. She had a sharp face made more severe by the way her straw-colored hair was yanked back into a ponytail. She paid no attention to Georgia or to the three younger children, a fat little boy whose legs stuck out almost straight from the sides of the Appaloosa, and two girls, about ten, who looked like twins. Georgia longed to make friends with them.

They were riding along at a slow walk, and all of the children except the oldest looked at Georgia with as much curiosity as she was looking at them.

Friends! she prayed. Other kids who like horses!

"Hi," she said.

The twins stopped chattering to each other and said, "Hi."

The older girl looked straight ahead, as if boredom were the only thing she could feel; and the little boy was too preoccupied with staying in the saddle to look up.

Georgia tried to think of something else to say, but before she could think of anything, the horses had passed her and she was enveloped in a thin cloud of dust stirred up by their feet. Well, she'd ask the Rosses who they were and how she could get to know them.

She checked the mailbox, not expecting anything and at the same time feeling a little shiver of dread that there might be a letter from her father: an angry letter demanding that they come home at once. Or else. "Or else" was something he used to say when he ordered her to do something. It was a small phrase to hold all the threat and unknown danger that it conveyed to her.

But there was no letter from him. Perhaps he didn't know yet where they were. She was sure the reason her mother had not had a phone put in was that it would be harder for him to find them.

There was a letter from a radio-TV store, urging the Occupant to come in for their fantastic end-of-month sale. That was all.

When she had fixed her sandwich, she went outside and sat on the tiny porch to eat it. The three kittens burst joyously out of the house and began to chase two leaves that had fallen from the willow tree. She was so interested in watching them, she didn't hear the approaching bike until the tires grated to a halt by the steps.

It was a girl she had seen at school. She hadn't yet sorted out many names, and she did not know this one. The girl was small and skinny, with glasses. She had a narrow, freckled face, and bright, interested eyes. Her bike fell onto the grass as she dropped it and came halfway up the steps.

"Hi," she said. "My name is Angela Fremont. I'm in your gym class and your English class. I live down that road . . ." She pointed toward the gravel road. ". . . and I'm curious to know where you come from. I heard you asking the teacher if you could do a theme on some composer. The only composers I know of are Simon and Garfunkel, and that's not the name you asked about."

"Puccini," Georgia said. "I asked her about Puccini."

"Who is that?"

"An Italian opera composer. He wrote *Madama Butterfly* and *The Girl of the Golden West* and a whole lot of other famous operas."

"What does an Italian know about the girl of the golden West?"

"Not much, I guess, but he based it on a play by an American, David Belasco."

"He sounds like an Italian, too."

"Well, the music is pretty." Georgia had the feeling she was losing an argument that she didn't know the point of.

"I never heard an opera." The statement seemed to say that if Angela Fremont had not heard opera, opera was not worth hearing.

Looking for a safer topic, Georgia said, "You like horses? I guess all western kids like horses so that's a dumb question."

"Not so dumb as assuming that all western kids like horses. I'm terrified of them. They give me asthma."

"Oh." Georgia felt defeated. "Would you like a Pepsi?"

She expected the girl to say that Pepsi turned her blue.

But instead Angela said, "Sure."

Georgia got up. "Would you look after the kittens for a minute? I mean like don't let them run away." Struck by a thought, she said, "Or do cats give you asthma?"

"No. Actually I prefer dogs, but I have nothing against cats."

When Georgia came back with the Pepsis, Angela was sitting on the floor and all three kittens were tumbling around in her lap. Angela watched them with clinical detachment, not touching them but not repulsing them either.

"I call them Ping, Pang, and Pong," Georgia said. She was prepared to explain the names, but Angela nodded as if Ping, Pang, and Pong were ordinary, familiar names for cats.

"Where's your mother?" Angela said, taking a long swig from the bottle.

"She's looking for a job. We just got here."

"Where's your father?"

Georgia hesitated. "He's still back East."

"Is he coming out here?"

She wished she could change the subject. "It depends. On his business and all."

Angela studied her. She took another long drink of Pepsi and burped. "You don't have to be self-conscious around me if your parents are divorced. My mother was divorced twice. I went through three fathers, and let me tell you, it goes from bad to worse. The guy I'm stuck with now is a beer swizzler."

"Swizzler?"

"Yeah. Soon as he gets home from work, he parks himself in front of the TV and swizzles beer. I can't even watch *Fame* any more, 'cause he's too cheap to pay for cable."

Georgia saw a common bond at last. "I love *Fame*, too."

"Well, you can't see it here without cable."

Remembering, Georgia said, "We can't see it anyway. We don't have our TV."

"Where is it?"

"Home."

Angela thought about it. "You seem to have a rather unusual and complicated situation here. No father but no divorce, no television, three cats, an unemployed mother, no horse but you're bound to get one, a bunch of facts about grand opera of all things . . . A really unusual situation."

Georgia didn't know whether to feel criticized or interesting. "I guess it's not all that unusual."

"Oh yes, it is. Definitely." She put down the empty Pepsi bottle and stood up, tumbling the kittens onto the floor of the porch. "See ya." And before Georgia could get her thoughts together, her guest had departed, doing wheelies down the gravel road with a fine disregard for her own safety.

8

IT WAS SNOWING. October had just begun, and it was snowing. It blew Georgia's mind. All along, of course, the peaks of the mountains had been snow-covered, but she had learned that they often stayed so all through the summer. This, however, was a true, ground-level snowstorm. The flakes melted as soon as they hit the ground, but they swirled around her like a real blizzard. She wasn't quite sure whether she was elated or alarmed. She had always loved the first snow-fall, but she was not mentally prepared for winter yet.

She tried to gather up enough snow for a snow-ball, but she couldn't manage it before the flakes melted in her hands. She turned her face toward the sky and felt the feathery touch. They were lighter than they seemed at home, drier. No wet east wind turned them to sleet. She knew her mother worried about winter, about driving into Missoula if she got a job there, about getting snowbound on this country road; but for the moment Georgia let all that slide off her mind and gave herself up to first snow excitement. If only Connie were here.

She picked up the kittens from the porch and held them up to the snow. "Snow," she told them. "Get used to it. There's a lot of it coming." She put them down, and except for a few seconds of shaking their front paws, Ping and Pang behaved as though they had always known snow. Pong, however, huddled close to Georgia's feet. Pong was the white one.

"Are you afraid you'll be mistaken for a snowball?" Georgia picked him up and cuddled him. "Don't worry. It melts." She let him lick a snowflake off her finger. "Back home," she told him, "the leaves are getting flaming red."

She took the kittens back into the kitchen and started down the road toward the Rosses' place. Her mother was still asleep. In the back of her mind that fact created a tiny, nagging worry. Her mother was usually an early riser, even on Saturdays. The only times Georgia had known her to sleep a lot was when things got really bad. Times when she felt so bad, she just didn't want to face the world.

But probably she was just tired. Saturday would not be a good day to job-hunt, and she must be beat after tramping all over Missoula and Stevensville and Hamilton day after day with nothing to show for it.

At least they were getting a phone on Monday. That made Georgia feel better, less like a displaced person or something. Her father had found out where they were anyway, Aunt Maisie said, possibly from the post office, although they weren't supposed to give it out. Georgia had a suspicion that Marge might have told him.

Georgia turned up the collar of her parka and wished she had remembered to snap on the hood. The snow melted on her skin and ran down the back of her neck.

The road looked empty. She almost wished she could see Angela swinging along in her funny sideways walk, one shoulder thrusting ahead like the bow of a boat. She was almost beginning to get used to Angela. She'd told her mother Angela was weird, and her mother had scolded her.

"People," she'd said, "who are different from other people are not necessarily weird. If you settled into an Eskimo village, you'd be the weird one."

She knocked on Mrs. Ross's door, and Elmore Ross, formerly only a dim profile in a pickup truck, faced her. He was wearing a black Stetson, old and shapeless and greasy, and it occurred to her that she had never seen him without it. For a second she wondered if he wore it to bed.

"Yeah?" he said, peering down at her. He had a beer can in his hand, and a faint trace of what looked like mustard on his chin.

She almost ran away, he looked so unwelcoming. But she was there, so she said, "I came to see Mrs. Ross.

Your mother," she added, in case he thought she didn't know that his wife was dead.

"I know who Mrs. Ross is." He jerked his head in a gesture that said, "Come in." "You'll find her in the kitchen, same as per usual." He wandered off in the direction of the television sounds that she could hear.

She hesitated a moment and then went in.

Mrs. Ross was sitting near the kitchen stove, her stockinged feet propped on another kitchen chair. In one hand she held a paperback mystery, and with the other she now and then shook an old-fashioned corn popper over the wood-burning stove. "There you are," she said, as if she had been expecting Georgia. "Why don't you shake this thing for me while I find out who done the English parson in." She passed the handle of the corn popper to Georgia. The corn was just beginning to jump, with small explosive pops. "You ever notice," Mrs. Ross went on, "how many of the clergy they always got mixed up in murders in English mysteries? Never came across one who done the horrid deed, but they do turn up as victims and detectives and innocent bystanders."

"I guess the rector or whatever is an important person in an English village," Georgia said.

"Well, wouldn't you think with all that piety, they'd be able to keep their flock from knocking each other off?" Mrs. Ross went on reading as she talked. Then she gasped, turned the page, and finally closed the book with a little pat. "She fooled me that time. I thought it was the greengrocer. How's the corn?"

"Popping like crazy." Georgia stood up and gave it a few last shakes. "Have you got a bowl or something?"

"On that shelf next to the sink. The blue bowl. There's butter melting in that little dipper. Not too much salt. I have to mind my salt. 'When the salt hath lost its savor, wherewith shall it be salted?' That never made a lick of sense to me. Do you know what it means?"

Georgia shook her head. She poured the melted butter carefully over the popped corn and handed Mrs. Ross the salt shaker. "You'd better do that part."

Mrs. Ross sprinkled the hot white kernels lightly, and then crammed a fistful into her mouth. "Mmm. I do love popcorn," she said with her mouth full.

"Me too." Georgia sat on the other side of the bowl, glad she'd come.

In a few minutes Marty came into the room, carrying a newspaper. "Thought I smelled popcorn."

"Help yourself," his grandmother said.

He stood with his back to the stove. "The Bigelows are moving for sure," he told her.

"Where to?"

"Some place in Utah."

"So you lose the horses."

"Right." He made a face. "Not all that much in it for me anyway, the way those brutes eat."

His grandmother gave him a quick glance. "Never mind, lad. There'll be other horses."

Georgia was listening intently. She ventured a question. "Are the Bigelows those kids that were boarding their horses?"

"Yup. Can't say I'm sorry to see the last of them, but I'll miss the critters." He took another handful of popcorn and cleared his throat. "Grandma..."

"Yes, I know, you got something on your mind. Spit it out, boy, spit it out."

"Well, there's a story in the paper about how they're rounding up another bunch of mustangs in the Pryor Mountains, and there's going to be a sale. I was thinkin', if I could get me maybe three or four and break 'em and sell 'em, I could clear a few bucks."

"How would you get them over here? Aren't the Pryor Mountains clear over there in the eastern part of the state?"

"No problem. I can borrow Joe Matteloch's horse trailer. In fact, Joe'd probably go over with me to help load and all."

"Got it all figured out, have you?" Mrs. Ross wiped a drop of butter from her chin.

"Well, no sense thinking of something if you don't know how you'd do it."

"And what you want from me is what they call down to the bank a capital investment."

He grinned. "Maybe I can see my way to cutting you in on a piece of the action."

They seemed to have forgotten that Georgia was there. She was sitting very still, listening to every word. In her mind she saw the horses he was talking about. She had read about the wild mustangs that the Bureau of Land Management rounded up and sold every now and then. In her imagination she saw a beautiful, strong, wild horse racing up a mountain, his mane and tail streaming out in the wind, his eyes intelligent and spirited, glowing with devotion to her, his best friend. She would tame him just enough so he could live in this world, and she would care for him all his days. Oh, the adventures they would have together!

She heard Mrs. Ross say, "I suppose I can see my way clear. As long as I don't have to go near 'em."

He laughed and rumpled her gray hair. "I wouldn't let you within a country mile of any horse of mine, Gran. When it comes to boats, you're just fine, but a horsewoman you ain't." He went out of the kitchen whistling.

On her way home Georgia remembered that she hadn't asked Marty how much he expected to sell his horses for. If she was going to scrape up the money somehow, she needed to know. It seemed like it wouldn't be an awful lot if they were wild and the government was selling them to take care of over-population.

She began to plan. She would ask Aunt Maisie to give her money for Christmas, maybe a little early? Her grandmother always gave her a check anyway. But maybe this year she wouldn't give her anything because she had left Grandmother's beloved son who could do no wrong.

She was glad to see the van in the yard. Her mother must have gotten up and gone out, maybe to the grocery store. Now she could tell her about the mustangs. She wouldn't bring up the subject of buying one yet though. Not while Mom was so worried about a job. Just plant the idea that there were going to be available horses, right next door practically. Mom liked Mrs. Ross a lot. That would help.

Oh, how wonderful it was going to be! It made her feel shaky just to think about it.

9

THERE WAS a letter on the kitchen table, addressed to her mother in her father's bold handwriting. The pages were spread out on the table, several of them, written all over with no margins. Miss Cassidy would never let him get away with that.

She found her mother in her bedroom, lying on her back, staring up at the ceiling. She had been crying. Georgia sat down on the bed. "Letter from Dad, huh?"

"Yes."

Georgia waited for her to say something more. "What'd he say?" she asked finally.

"You can read it if you want. Lots of complaining. Lots of threats."

Georgia put her hand on her mother's arm. "Mom, he can't hurt us."

Her mother gave her a wan smile. "He can sure shake us up though." She sat up abruptly. "Well, enough of this. How's the snow?"

"It's quit. Most of it's melted. You want me to fix you a cup of tea?"

"I'd love it." Her mother was sounding brisk, as if she were determined not to be depressed. She combed her short, wavy brown hair and put on the blue sweat shirt that made her eyes look very blue. She looks like me, Georgia thought, watching her in the mirror. No, I look like her. She used to wish she looked like her dark, handsome father, but now she was just as glad she didn't.

She made the tea for her mother and got herself a glass of orange juice. Sitting down across the table from her mother, she glanced quickly through her father's letter, and then put it back in the envelope. Now she had to think about him instead of the mustangs. He always spoiled everything.

"How did school go?" her mother said, and then she laughed, remembering it was Saturday. "Don't mind me. I'm getting absentminded in my old age."

"You've got a lot on your mind."

"You can say that again." Her mother poured herself some more tea. "I got the paper when I was out. There are a few possibilities. I'm going into Missoula later to see about them. Do you want to go?"

"Sure." Anything to change the scene.

On the way, she told her mother about Marty's

[49]

plan for the mustangs. Her mother gave her a quick look, but she didn't say much except, "What is a mustang exactly?"

"Horses that live in the wild. They're descended from Spanish horses a long time ago and horses that ran away from the Cavalry, and I guess from the Indians."

"They'd be hard to tame."

"Oh, I guess if you gave them plenty of love and care, it wouldn't be so hard."

Her mother changed the subject. "How is Vera Ross?"

"She's fine. She told me to tell you about the laundromat. She said you wanted to know. It's part of an old motel up on the highway. She'll take me after school Monday." She had been watching the wide, slow-moving Bitter Root River, winding along below the highway. Now she looked back at her mother and was struck with how thin and tired she looked. "You aren't worried about Dad making all those threats, are you? Like killing himself?"

"It makes me feel guilty."

"He's just trying to make you guilty. He isn't about to hurt himself. He's too spoiled."

Her mother gave a sad laugh. "I guess you understand him better than I do."

"Maybe I'm like him." Georgia's words startled herself. What an idea! Could it be true?"

"No, you're not, Georgia. You're right up front. I trust you."

She sighed with relief. It was good to know your mother trusted you. It gave you an extra responsibility though. Like if she was going to have a horse, it was up to her to do it herself.

Her mother let her off at the Southgate Mall, and she wandered around the shops feeling as if she were back in a city.

When her mother met her under the clock in the mall, she was smiling all over her face. "You're not going to believe it," she said to Georgia.

"You got a job!"

"You'd better believe it!"

Georgia gave a whoop of joy, and several people nearby smiled at her. "What doing?"

"Waitress. Late afternoons and evenings."

"Oh." She felt a pang of dismay. Waitressing was low-paid hard work.

Her mother laughed. She looked years younger. "Don't tell me I'm underemployed." That was what her father was always saying about himself. "It's a very nice Mexican-American restaurant, owned and managed by a German couple. They're really nice. The place does a big dinner trade."

"How's the pay?"

"Waitresses never make a fortune, but there'll be tips. And it's a job, sweetheart, an honest-to-God job, with money! We can pay the rent, buy groceries."

"Where is it?"

"Downtown Missoula. Right in the heart of things. Oh, George, we can lift up our heads again."

[51]

Georgia felt suddenly very moved by her mother's courage. "I love you, Mom."

"I love you, too. Let's go buy you a new album."

So it was going to be all right. Things were looking up.

"*Norma*," she said. "Could we get *Norma*, with Sutherland and Marilyn Horne?"

"You bet we can."

"And the new Robert Parker for you," Georgia said, as they came to the B. Dalton store. She felt pleased with herself for remembering that Mom should get something for herself. Maybe she was growing up. Was that what adversity did to you?

10

FOR THE SECOND TIME on a Monday afternoon Georgia put her laundry basket into the back of Vera Ross's ancient Chevy, and they drove to the little laundromat. It was one of several old wooden buildings attached to the motel. It didn't look like a laundry on the outside, but inside, the machines hummed and the air was warm and moist and soapy like any city laundromat.

There were several women ahead of them, and all the machines and the few chairs were full. The women all greeted Vera by name; and one of them, a Mrs. Delahue, fussed and carried on over her as if, Mrs. Ross later said to Georgia, she were some kind of relic, ready for National Preservation.

Finally two washing machines were free, and when Mrs. Ross had loaded her laundry into one of them, Mrs. Delahue patted her shoulder and said in her patronizing voice, "There you are, dear. Now you sit right down over here, so you won't get wore out."

Mrs. Ross gave her a blinding smile and said through her teeth, "You pat me again, Mabel Delahue, and I'll bite your head off."

Mrs. Delahue's eyes flew wide open, but the other women laughed, and she decided to laugh too, but she was offended.

When she had gone, Georgia said, "You're wicked."

"I know," Mrs. Ross said. "But I do hate to be patted. Now then, I got some news for you. Marty's leaving in the morning to see about those wild horses."

Georgia gasped. "He is?"

"We was wondering, maybe you'd like one? He'll break it, of course. He said you was looking for a horse."

"Oh, I'd love one. I can't tell you how much. But I don't have any money."

"I suspected that. Your mother's talked to me some. Maybe we could make a deal. I need somebody to help me around the house." She made a face. "You can see from Mabel Delahue what a weak good-for-nothing old woman I am."

"But you aren't."

"No, I'm not. But I got arthritis, and there's a lot of things it's painful for me to do. I could use help. You want to work out your horse?"

Georgia's heart was thumping. "Of course I do. But I don't know what my mom'll say."

"Talk to her. Let me know."

Georgia slumped back in her chair, staring unseeingly at the waves of soapy water that sloshed against the glass front of the washing machine. In her mind she was seeing a sleek, beautiful black stallion, racing across wide spaces toward the horizon. His mane flowed in the wind, and his neck was arched. She was riding him.

That night she could hardly wait for her mother to get home. She made coffee for her and sliced some of the cake her mother had brought home the day before. She waited impatiently for the sound of the van.

Her mother looked surprised. "What are you doing up? It's late." She looked tired, but her face these days was more relaxed. The little frown of worry was gone.

Georgia waited till her mother sipped the coffee. "I've got a job!"

Her mother looked up in surprise. "Tell me."

She explained about Vera Ross's offer, then watched her mother anxiously. What if she didn't think it was a good idea?

After a minute her mother said, "They're good people, the Rosses."

"Then it's okay?"

"I don't see why not. If you won't get too tired with schoolwork and all."

Georgia leaped out of her chair and hugged her mother. "I'm going to repair our corral. It's all falling down. And I'll clean out the barn. There are two stalls in there."

"I've never even looked in the barn. Can the horse stay at the Rosses' while he's being tamed?"

"Sure. Marty will break him but I'll help. He'll show me how." Marty hadn't said that, but she knew he would.

"Well, just promise you'll be careful. I don't suppose a wild horse is much like those riding school creatures you used to ride."

Georgia was so excited, it took her a long time to get to sleep. She would write Connie tomorrow and tell her all about it. And somewhat to her surprise, she found she couldn't wait to tell Angela.

11

ANGELA HAD TAKEN to dropping in quite often after school. She seldom stayed long, but Georgia had found herself more and more looking forward to her visits.

On the day after the excitement about the mustang, she waited impatiently. If Angela didn't come, she would go to her house. Only she didn't really know where Angela lived. Only the road, and there were half a dozen small houses and farms along that dirt road. Angela had never asked her over.

She sat on the front steps trying to keep her mind on her history homework, but looking up expectantly every time she heard a sound on the road. A milk truck went by. A pickup. A boy on a bike.

When Angela came, it was, as always, with such speed that Georgia didn't become aware of her until she was pedaling into the yard. She threw down her bike and sat on the steps. "Who is Thomas Paine, and why do we have to know?"

"Listen, never mind Thomas Paine. I've got news."

"What?"

"I'm getting a horse!"

Angela sneezed. "Hey, that's wonderful, really. Only . . ." She sneezed again, long and loud.

"I forgot. You're allergic. Even to the *word*?"

"Allergies are . . ." Sneeze. ". . . partly mental." She found a bedraggled Kleenex in her pocket and blew her nose. "But hey, that's great, no kidding. I'm real glad."

"You'll still come to see me, won't you?"

" 'Course I will. You need to fix up that corral, I guess."

"Yes, I do."

"Well, I can hammer nails faster than anybody you know."

"You mean you'll help?"

"Sneezing and blowing all the way. Anything for a friend." Angela made a wide dramatic gesture with her arm.

"That's really nice. I mean I really appreciate it."

"Well, let's don't waste time in chitchat. Have you got a hammer?" She jumped up and ran out to the corral.

"Some of these posts are rotten." Angela kicked at a fallen post, sending a cloud of sawdust into the air. She whipped a small notebook and pencil out of her jeans pocket. "We better make notes as we go."

"Are posts expensive?"

"Yes, but don't buy any. We've got some at our place just lying around. Stepfather number two thought he was a cowboy."

Georgia found a fallen post that seemed solid, and she tried to fit it into the hole it had once been set in.

"Wait," Angela said. "We need a posthole digger. You got a posthole digger?"

Georgia giggled. "Oh, sure, I got a set of 'em. In decorator colors. Angela, what would I be doing with a posthole digger?"

"Maybe in the barn." Angela trotted off and came back a few minutes later carrying a rusty spade, a pitchfork, and a crowbar. "No posthole digger. Too bad." She went at the half-filled hole with the crowbar and then with the spade, shoveling the hard dirt out of the depression.

Georgia felt helpless. She needed something to do. So she went out to the middle of the corral and checked on the snubbing post. That was where she would stand when she was training her horse.

She put her hand on the rough wood and saw herself guiding her beautiful Sky around and around in graceful circles. He would learn fast. She would be very patient with him. Marty said if a horse got scared once, he never forgot it the rest of his life. She would make sure he never got scared. She saw herself gently putting the saddle on his back. And Marty saying, "Hey, that horse of yours has shaped up real nice. You can ride him anywhere." She hadn't thought to ask how long it took to break a horse.

"Quit dreaming and come help me." Angela was struggling with a post, trying to make it stand in the hole while she shoveled in the loose dirt and tamped it down.

"I was planning," Georgia said.

"Well, plan yourself right over here. Hold that thing steady while I whack it further into the hole."

"Don't hit my hands," Georgia said.

"Nobody's going to hit your hands. Hold steady now."

Georgia flinched as the back of the spade came down hard on the post. She felt the shock in her hands. Three more blows, and it was in far enough to suit Angela.

"Now get out of the way before you get a shovelful of dirt all over those good dude pants."

Georgia stood back and watched Angela attacking the posthole. For a skinny kid, Angela had a lot of muscle. Georgia had pretty good muscles herself, but she didn't think she could do what Angela was doing. She looked at her friend with new respect. They'd have to do a lot of work, though, if the corral was going to be ready for Sky. She'd need to clear out the stall, too. It had been used by the owners of the place as a catch-all for worn-out tires, rusty tools, empty gasoline cans. People sure did hate to throw things away.

An hour later Georgia went into the house and came back with two Diet Pepsis and her transistor radio. Angela sat on the hard ground and drank thirstily from the bottle. Her short blonde braid was coming unplaited, and her glasses had slid halfway down her nose. The white kitten climbed her arm and tried to drink out of the bottle.

"Shoo, Pong," she said, but she didn't push the kitten away.

Ping and Pang were chasing a beetle that was trying to find an escape route under Georgia's ankle.

"Do you know Ping and Pang apart?" Georgia said.

"Sure. That's Ping, with the kink in her tail."

Georgia was impressed. Her mother could never tell them apart, and sometimes she wasn't sure herself about Ping and Pang. She hadn't noticed that tiny kink. "How come you don't like horses if you like cats?"

Angela's eyes widened. "There's about as much sameness between a cat and a horse as there is between a spidermonkey and a gorilla."

"Oh." Georgia wasn't sure what a spidermonkey was, but she was not about to ask. Angela never seemed to have doubts about anything. What she knew, she knew. It would be nice to be like that.

They sprawled in the hot sun, enjoying the Indian summer. The radio was playing a pop recording.

"He's so super," Georgia said dreamily.

"Who is?"

"Billy Joel." The recording reminded her of her own room at home.

"Who's he?" Angela picked up Pong and held him so close to her face that the kitten and the girl were staring at each other almost cross-eyed.

Georgia couldn't believe that Angela didn't know who Billy Joel was. The announcer answered the question for her.

"That was Billy Joel," he said. "And I've got an announcement of a lost dog."

Angela sat up abruptly and listened.

"A miniature dachsund, answers to the name of Fred, two years old, wearing a rabies tag, lost somewhere near the Florence post office. If you find Fred, give us a call here, or call . . ."

Angela grabbed her little pad of paper and wrote down the phone number that he was reading off. She set Pong on the ground and got to her feet. "See you later. Thanks for the Pepsi."

"Where are you going?" Georgia always felt startled by the speed with which Angela moved.

"Got to see if I can find the lost dog."

"Why? Do you know him?"

Angela was already leaving. "I always look for 'em. I got three at home now." She ran across the yard toward her bicycle.

"But Florence is seven or eight miles . . ."

Angela didn't bother to answer. She waved, grabbed her bike, and sped off down the road.

"Well!" Georgia said. She brushed the kittens aside and began to gather up the tools. Connie would never dash off and leave her like that. But then, she thought, Connie would never have spent an hour digging postholes either. Miss Cassidy said that Ralph Waldo Emerson said that there were compensations. Maybe so. Sometime she'd have to sit down and add up two columns in her journal: The Good Things Back Home, and The Good Things Out West. Maybe they'd come out even. Right now though it was hard to think of anything back home that would balance Sky.

She stacked the tools in a corner of the barn and swept the stall to get out the worst of the rubbish. It would be a while before Sky moved in, but she wanted to be ready.

She stood back, sweaty and tired, looking at the clean stall. "That's where my horse is going to live. My horse. Sky." She wished Marty Ross would hurry.

12

"YOU GOT that old den so clean, it hurts my eyes,"
Mrs. Ross said. "Come, sit down and have a cup of
tea."

In the big, comfortable kitchen Georgia sat back
and sipped the tea called "Evening in Missoula" that
Mrs. Ross liked. It was spicy and refreshing, not like
ordinary tea at all. There was nothing ordinary about
Mrs. Ross.

"How's your mama doin' at that restaurant?"

"Pretty good. She gets awfully tired, but the
people are nice."

"You had any meals over there? They know how
to make a decent enchilada?"

"I haven't been there, but Mom has brought
home food a few times. Cheese enchiladas, chile rel-
lenos, empanadas . . . They're real good."

"Mmm." Mrs. Ross smacked her lips. "I do like good hot Mexican food."

"Maybe you'd come have supper with us some Monday. Mom doesn't work Mondays. She's learning to cook Mexican, and she's real good."

"I'll be there with bells on."

Georgia smiled. "Good." She had grown very fond of Vera Ross. And it would be good for her mother to have company. Georgia could help with the cooking. She didn't like to say so, but she wasn't too bad a cook herself.

"My husband and I lived in Texas one time, for a couple of years. I got a taste for jalapenos that I never got over."

"You've had an interesting life."

"Any life is interesting if you work up enough steam to get interested in it. Being bored comes from inside a person. Maybe from the liver, I don't know; or the pancreas. Never was too sure what the pancreas was for." She looked out the window as the wind blew a branch against the side of the house. "I keep thinking I hear that young 'un coming home."

It took Georgia a moment to realize that she meant Marty. She didn't think of him as a young 'un. "Me too," she said. "I can't wait to see my horse."

"Hope he don't get into trouble." The old woman was frowning, staring unseeingly out the window.

"Marty? Oh, he wouldn't get into trouble."

Mrs. Ross gave her a quick glance. "Hope you're

right, child. Have some more tea. And there's plenty of that cake, so dig right in."

Later Georgia thought how odd it was that both of them had been starting at every sound, expecting it to be Marty, and when he really came, neither of them heard him until the big horse trailer crunched on the gravel just outside the kitchen window.

"He's here!" Georgia almost dropped her tea-cup. She jumped to her feet, spilling cookie crumbs on the clean floor. "Vera, Marty's here."

"So I see." Vera Ross got up slowly, as if she were not in the least excited, but her face had changed. She looked relaxed and smiling. "With all those wild critters."

Georgia stayed on the back steps, hugging her-self to keep from leaping at the horse trailer to see Sky. Without anything more than a quick wave at his grandmother, Marty jumped down from the pas-senger's side of the cab, and he and his friend Joe Mat-teloch went around to the back of the trailer. A horse whinnied and stamped his foot. She could just see the tops of their heads from where she stood, but she was afraid she would get in the way if she went closer.

She heard the clunk of the trailer gate opening, and a moment later Joe came around the far side of the truck, leading a horse. As they came into Geor-gia's view, she let out her breath in a gasp of shock. The horse, who was fighting the rope, was small, chunky, with a patchy coat, clumps of thick fur alter-nating with bare spots, as if he were motheaten. His heavy mane fell long on both sides, and his tail was long and unkempt.

It couldn't be Sky. She looked at the next horse, which Marty was trying to lead toward the stable. This one was a mare, a buckskin, and if possible a worse-looking horse than the first. Her ears were flat to her head, and her baleful eyes showed the whites, as she fought the lead. Against the buckskin coat, a tangled black mane and a black stripe down her back and black hooves made her look almost like a clown. Her withers were high and bony, and her untrimmed feet splayed forward in long, grotesque upward curves like elfin shoes.

She stood riveted to the steps as Marty and Joe unloaded the other two horses. The last one fought the rope so violently that he nearly broke away. Joe was dragged along the ground, digging in his heels and struggling to bring the mustang under control.

When Marty and Joe finally had all four horses in their stalls, Joe climbed into the cab and turned the rig in a slow, wide circle. He blew his horn twice, waved at Marty, and drove away, the empty horse trailer bouncing behind him.

Marty's jeans were torn and his shirt was filthy. He had a long streak of dirt down the side of his face. But he stood with his hands on his hips, grinning, in front of Georgia and his grandmother.

"Well! Ain't they a pretty bunch?"

Vera Ross looked worried. "It was a crazy scheme. They're wild, boy."

" 'Course they're wild. How else would I get four horses for three hundred bucks?"

"And you got to feed 'em all winter."

"Don't worry about it." He looked at Georgia. "Yours is the buckskin. How do you like her?"

Georgia couldn't speak. He had made a fool of her. He had stuck her with an ugly, bad-tempered little runt of a horse. And she had been working so hard and hoping so long . . . She thought of the Arab with flowing mane and arched neck that she had imagined. If she tried to answer him, she would burst into tears, and she was not going to give him that satisfaction. She jumped off the steps and ran down the drive toward the road. She heard Mrs. Ross call, but she didn't slow down.

When she got home, she threw herself on her bed and cried for a long time.

13

SHE THOUGHT about not going to school the next day. She had cried so much during the night that her head ached. And she just didn't feel like facing people. Since her mother had started work, Georgia often got her own breakfast so her mother could sleep late. It would be easy enough just not to go to school. But then she would have to explain, and she wasn't ready to talk to her mother yet about the horse. She had to figure out first what she was going to do. Maybe she could sell it back to Marty, but she couldn't talk to him yet; she was too hurt and angry that he would trick her like that. He had known what wild mustangs were like, and he had let her think it would be a good horse.

She went to school after all, but she stayed away from everyone, especially Angela. She saw Angela's hurt look when she ducked away, but she couldn't help it. Sometime she'd have to explain but not now. Maybe later she could turn it all into a joke. Some joke.

The minute she walked into the house after school, her mother said, "What's the matter?"

Georgia tried the headache story, but her mother said, "You've been crying. What is it?"

She told her about the mustangs. "Marty played me for a sucker," she said bitterly, at the end of her story.

Her mother put her hand over Georgia's. "I'm really sorry about the horse. I know how you've counted on it. But I don't really think Marty meant to fool you."

"Then why didn't he tell me what those horses were like?"

"Maybe he didn't know."

"He knew."

"Or maybe he thought you knew. You were so busy imagining your own horse, honey, perhaps you weren't paying much attention to what the reality might be. I don't think you should blame Marty. At least talk to him about it."

"I don't want to go over there again."

Her mother was silent for a minute. "You have an agreement with Vera. Marty brought that horse for you. You owe Vera."

"Not if it was a fraud."

Her mother got up and put the tea kettle on the stove. "It wasn't a fraud. You know the Rosses better than that. You made a bargain, dear. You must carry it out, or else make some other fair arrangement with Vera."

Georgia picked up the white kitten and went out into the back yard. She walked to the unfinished corral. There was no point in finishing it now. Angela would probably be mad, to have done all that work for nothing. "I'll end up with no friends at all," Georgia said to the kitten. "Only you and your sisters."

The kitten settled on her shoulder and purred in her ear.

"But you're not a horse."

When it was time for her to go to the Rosses', to clean for Vera, she went, but she had to force herself along every step of the way.

As she came into the yard, she could hear heavy pacing from the stable. It sounded as if a whole herd of horses were stomping angrily up and down in their stalls. She didn't envy Marty the job of breaking horses like those.

Mrs. Ross gave her a searching look when she came into the kitchen. Georgia hadn't decided what she wanted to say. It wasn't Vera Ross's fault, after all. She said hi and got the vacuum cleaner out of the back hall.

"Hold on a minute," Mrs. Ross said, as Georgia started to go into the front hall. "Sit a minute."

Georgia propped the vacuum cleaner against the wall, and it promptly fell down with a clatter. It was old, and the mechanism for holding the handle upright didn't work. She picked it up and leaned it more securely against the door jamb.

"I ought to get me one of those new Hoovers," Vera Ross said. "That old thing's about had it. You want a piece of rhubarb pie?"

"No, thanks," Georgia said.

"How come?"

"Well, I have a lot of homework. I need to get my work done and go home. Thanks just the same."

"Made it this morning." Mrs. Ross studied the pie, as if looking for possible flaws. "You kind of disappointed at that cayuse of yours?"

Georgia bit her lip. "Kind of." Tears stung her throat. She tried to fight them back.

"That's what we figured. I told Marty he should have described 'em. You never seen a wild horse before, did you?"

"No."

"I should have given it more thought. You want to get rid of it?"

"How can I? I'm committed."

"Lord, child, you aren't committed till you're dead."

"I made an arrangement with you. You paid him for my horse. I have to work it out."

"First of all, you can sell it back to him. Second, you don't have to work for me unless you want to. This is no slave market. If you don't want the horse but you want to work, I'll pay you in cash instead of horseflesh, that's all. I like having you here. You get the house clean, and you're company. But you are no way obliged."

"Mom says I am." It was turning out differently than she had expected. She wasn't sure what to say.

"Why don't you go on out to the stable and have a talk with Marty? He's the horse merchant. Take another look at your horse; maybe she won't look quite so bad today. But talk it out with him, one way or another. Marty's fair."

Georgia took a deep breath. "All right." She didn't want to, but she knew she had to.

He was currying the buckskin when she came into the stable. The little horse had her head twisted around, watching him with obvious suspicion. Her ears flicked up and down, and her long tail switched restlessly. The other horses craned their necks to look at Georgia. The dusty black stallion, the one who had almost escaped, rolled his eyes and pawed at the floor of the stall. One of the others gave a sharp neigh that made Georgia jump.

"Hi," Marty said, glancing up. "I'm trying to get this baby to lookin' civilized, but it ain't easy."

The buckskin did look better. He had trimmed her mane and her tail and combed and curried her. There was no way he could cover the patchy bare spots, but she did look cleaner and neater. Of course, she was still an ugly, mean-looking runt.

"What you going to call her?"

"Nothing," Georgia said. "I don't want her."

He gave her another quick look, but then he went

on as if he hadn't heard her. "What was it? Sky? Was that what you said? That's a good name. Jed Dubois's coming over tomorrow to do something about their feet. Trim 'em up. Did you ever see such ugly hooves in your life?"

"No," Georgia said, "I never did. I never saw such ugly horses."

He laughed. "Beauty is as beauty does. These little devils are stronger than a team of Clydesdales. And you ought to see them climb! Like mountain goats. Real smart, these babies. They have to be, to survive." He jerked his arm back as the buckskin tried to nip him. "Hold on, there, young Sky. Don't get smart with me." He slapped her hindquarters and she sidestepped nervously. "You and me's got a long way to go before you're ready for Georgia, young Sky, but we'll make it." He stepped out of the stall, locked the gate, and put away the curry comb. "You feeling kind of depressed about her?" he said to Georgia.

"Yes," Georgia said.

His face was serious now. "You don't have to take her if you don't want. If you think she's going to be too much for you."

Georgia was indignant. "It's not that. She just isn't what I expected."

"What'd you expect? You knew it was a wild horse you were getting. Did you think she'd be all groomed and pretty and ready to carry your ladyship all over the place? In an eastern saddle? Jodphurs? Silver-headed riding crop? One of them black velvet crash helmets, like the English wear? Is that what you thought? Steeplechasing, maybe? Polo games?"

"You think you're so smart," she said.

He shrugged. "I thought you was smart, too. Now I ain't so sure." He turned away. "But I'll buy her back from you. She's the best one of the lot. You work it out with Grandma. She's the treasurer of this outfit."

She couldn't let him get away with this. "You think I'm scared of her, don't you."

"What else is there to think?"

"You think I'm a dumb eastern dude."

"You said it, I didn't." He had his back to her now.

"Well, you'd better not try selling her to anyone else. She's my horse, you know."

"Yeah, but you don't want her."

"I'm the one to decide that." She marched out of the stable and back to the house. She picked up the vacuum cleaner without looking at Mrs. Ross.

Later when she had finished, she found Mrs. Ross kneading bread dough. Georgia put the cleaner in the back hall without speaking.

"What's the new arrangement?" Vera said.

"There isn't any new arrangement," Georgia said.

"Oh. You want a piece of that rhubarb pie now?"

"Yes, please." Georgia sat down at the table. There was an ugly little mutt of a horse out there in the stable, and her name was Sky. It was not what

Georgia had dreamed of or wanted, but she wasn't going to let Vera Ross down, and she was not about to let Marty think she was scared. She would ride Sky if it was the last thing she did. And maybe, she thought grimly, it will be.

14

SHE HEARD the phone ring and glanced at her clock. Saturday morning at eight o'clock? Who would call so early? Faintly she heard her mother's voice. So it was not for her. She turned over and tried to go back to sleep. But that darned horse was on her mind. What could she possibly do with her? Maybe she could help Marty train her, and then she could sell her, the way he planned to sell his. It didn't seem likely anybody would want to pay more than a few dollars for her, though.

She got up, deciding she might as well take another look at her freaky horse. When she arrived downstairs, her mother had gone back to her room. She got awfully tired at the restaurant. It worried Georgia. She fixed herself some breakfast and made a pot of coffee for her mother. There was a letter on the kitchen table from Marge to her mother. Marge kept pressuring them to come home. Georgia couldn't understand why she was interfering, since she was never home herself. Maybe Dad had talked her into it. Well, they would never go.

She walked down the road to the Rosses' barn and leaned on Sky's stall door. The horse and Georgia stared at each other, Sky twisting her head around to get a good look.

"You don't look all that thrilled to see me," Georgia said. "Well, if you must know, I'm not all that thrilled with you. But we're stuck with each other, so we're going to have to be friends if it kills us."

Sky nickered and tossed her head.

Marty came out from the house. " 'Morning."

"Good morning."

"How does she look to you today?"

"Terrible."

He laughed. "Better not say that. You'll hurt her feelings." He went into the stall and unhitched Sky. "Let's go for a walk, old girl," he said to her.

Georgia hastily got out of the way as Sky came stomping out, but she followed the two to the corral to watch. Marty showed her the soft webbed longeing rein. "See, I loop this under her tail." He went out to the snubbing post and encouraged the horse to circle around the corral. Sky started and stopped as she chose.

Georgia hung on the fence and watched. After a while he changed to a lariat.

"It's got a little more bite to it. Make her pay attention."

"Will it hurt her?"

"No."

But Sky wasn't responding to Marty's efforts. As Georgia watched, feeling drowsy in the clear cold sunlight, Marty tried a light pull on the hackamore. Sky jerked hard, and suddenly Marty was sitting on the cold ground.

Sky craned her neck to look at him, and for a crazy moment Georgia could have sworn the little mustang was laughing.

Marty got up and dusted himself off. "You let a horse outsmart you once and you got trouble getting her out of that notion. Har!" He stomped his foot and then led the horse around the ring until Georgia was ready to fall over with boredom. She didn't want a horse that was just going to walk in circles. Maybe they ought to turn her loose up in the canyon and let her go back to her wild ways.

After a while she went home. She found her mother and Angela stringing beans in the kitchen.

"Angela brought us the last beans of the season."

Georgia didn't feel like talking to Angela, or anyone. She still felt sore and bruised inside because she had counted so much on her horse, and it had turned out to be an ugly little monster who didn't even like her.

Her mother and Angela seemed to have gotten

very well acquainted. They acted as if they had secrets. In Georgia's present state of mind, she suspected they were in league against her, somehow. She knew that was silly, but that was how she felt, like an outsider. She sat, brooding and silent, watching them work and laugh and talk.

"There's going to be a concert at Christmas," Angela said to her.

"I know that." Georgia had ears. It had been announced in school, after all.

"You ought to try out."

"Why don't you, dear?" her mother said.

"I don't want to." She knew she sounded sulky and she wasn't proud of herself. She wanted to go up to her room, but if she did, her mother would scold her for being rude.

"You practice real hard, don't you," Angela said.

It seemed to Georgia that Angela looked at her as if she were some kind of oddball. "You can't be a singer if you don't practice."

Angela laughed as if she had said something funny, and then she did a crazy scale, offkey. Georgia's mother laughed. Georgia felt as if the two of them belonged to some club she didn't even know about.

To change the subject, Georgia said, "I've never met your mother."

"I hardly know her socially myself."

Georgia stared at her. "Angela, you're weird."

Then she remembered that her mother objected to that kind of statement. "How come you never ask me over to your house?"

"I'm afraid you'd come."

The best thing was to laugh it off. Assume that Angela was kidding, although she looked perfectly serious. "I'm going to work on the corral for an hour," she said.

"Have fun," Angela said, and went on stringing beans.

Georgia couldn't believe that Angela wouldn't join her. Was she mad or something? No matter what her mother said, Angela was really weird.

Later, when she came in to get a Band-Aid for the thumb she had hit with her hammer, she said as much to her mother. Angela was gone. "Why did she act like that?"

"You weren't terribly cordial to her, sweetheart. Anyway, I think she really did have to go home. And Georgia, don't invite yourself to somebody else's house, please. Have enough faith in your friend to believe she has her reasons."

Georgia felt unjustly accused, and that was one of her least favorite things to feel. Her mother ought to see how strange Angela was. And Georgia hadn't been inviting herself to Angela's house; she had just been asking why she was never invited. It seemed logical to invite your new friend to come to your house, didn't it?

"Doesn't it seem logical," she said, "that she would invite me to her house? She comes here all the time."

"Do you invite her?"

"No, she just drops by."

"Well, if you're so anxious to see where she lives, why don't you drop by? I suppose there's no great harm in that, as long as you don't barge into the house."

"I don't barge into houses," Georgia said stiffly.

Her mother smiled. "Don't get huffy, darling. Nobody's against you."

Georgia was not so sure of that, but she tried not to be huffy. Aunt Maisie had said in a letter, "Be good to your mother." It was her responsibility. And Aunt Maisie was a good friend. She had even checked up on Cinders and reported that the cat was dining sumptuously on Dinners for Finicky Eaters and real chicken livers. Georgia picked up Ping and Pang. They were growing. Maybe she ought to buy them some chicken livers.

15

GEORGIA OFFERED to feed and water her horse or whatever needed to be done, but Marty suggested she stay away for a few days.

"Give me time to psych her out."

So it was nearly a week before she went back again to the barn. She had just finished waxing Mrs. Ross's kitchen floor, and she couldn't resist taking a look at what Vera called the cayuse before she went home.

Marty handed her the lead rope. "Take her around."

"She'll bolt." Sky was already rolling her eyes at Georgia, showing the whites.

"Don't let her."

Georgia was scared. She could picture herself jerked off her feet, still hanging onto the rope and bouncing along on the hard ground. But she started guiding the buckskin around the corral, and to her astonishment, the horse obeyed as meekly as an old riding club horse at home. But Georgia was not fooled. She was aware of the muscle power at the other end of that rope. Still, by the time she gave the horse back to Marty, she was feeling good.

"Maybe I should get a little whip," she said. "Not to hurt her, but just to show her, impress her."

"No, don't ever do that," Marty said. "This kind of horse, I would never use a whip or even let her see one. She's too jumpy. I don't go much for whip-breaking anyhow."

That night Georgia told her mother that her mustang was beginning to show signs of having some sense.

The next day as Marty again handed Georgia the hackamore, Sky suddenly tore the line out of Georgia's hands and raced around and around the ring at a full gallop. It took Marty several busy minutes to get things under control. He grinned ruefully at Georgia.

"I guess this ain't one of her better days."

"No." Georgia looked at the rope burns on her hand. "She'll never get broken."

But for the first time Georgia had a real urge to make her horse shape up. All the rest of the week she went back when Marty was there and worked with Sky. Things began to get better.

"You and me," she said to Sky, "are beginning to communicate."

Sky put her ears back and swished her tail.

"Don't sass me back now. We're going to work out a relationship." Georgia put her hand on Sky's neck and felt the muscles quiver. It was like touching something electric.

That night when her mother got home, she was still awake, planning maneuvers to try with Sky. "I think that horse might be ridable some day after all," she said.

"Wonderful." Her mother sounded bone weary. She sank into a kitchen chair and took off her shoes. "We had the overflow of a convention crowd. What a hassle!"

"Did you get a lot of tips?"

Her mother shrugged. "Not all that much. We never seem to have quite enough to get ahead, do we."

"You aren't sorry we came, are you?" Georgia felt sudden alarm.

"I guess not. But if I'd known how hard it was going to be, I don't think I'd have had the guts."

"I could sell the horse back to Marty, and that way I'd have the money Mrs. Ross pays me for household expenses." It surprised her to find that so difficult to say.

Her mother patted her hand. "No, you keep your horse. We'll manage."

I wouldn't have believed it, Georgia thought after she had gone to bed, that it would be hard to give up that crazy little mustang. Sky's so ornery, no matter who owned her, she'd still be looking for a way to break out and run free.

[85]

When Marty got a job with a rancher, he had to confine his work with the mustangs to the short daylight hours left when he got home. Georgia did what she could to help, trying not to get in the way. The horses grazed over the fifteen fenced acres of the Ross place, and one of Georgia's jobs was to help catch the one that Marty was going to work with in the corral.

She learned how to mix the food supplement and to get the hose and fill the watering trough. When he took the horses into the stable to brush them down, she helped.

Sky was looking a little better. Her hooves had been trimmed. The patchy places in her coat were growing in. Sometimes Georgia got the currycomb and worked on her mane. Marty had trimmed it, and he had combed and trimmed most of the hair out of the bushy tail. He had even mixed up some bluing and combed it into her mane until it gleamed black as ebony. But there was nothing they could do about Sky's size or her bony structure. She would always be an ugly little runt.

In early November Marty tried putting a blanket on Sky's back, then taking it off a moment later. He did it several times. "I want to get her used to something on her back. Tomorrow I'm going to try a saddle."

"She'll buck it off."

"Maybe. But we got to start some time."

Georgia, herself, sensed a change in the horse. When she had her on the rope, she didn't get the feeling that an explosion was about to go off. Maybe Sky was calming down a little.

Marty tried the blanket again and again until Sky let it stay on her back without paying any attention to it. He explained to Georgia about putting on a saddle. "Don't leave the stirrups banging, or the cinch strap or the latigo flapping. She'll spook at anything like that that she can't see."

When it grew too dark to work, he took the horse into the stable for a brushdown. Georgia worked on the other side. Clouds of dust rose from the mustang's coat. Georgia sneezed, and Sky's muscles quivered.

Marty bent over one of her hind hooves. "She's got some little tiny cracks in her hooves. I had a horse got them one time, and I put Crazy Glue on 'em. Kept 'em from spreading."

Georgia laughed. "Crazy Glue?"

"Sure."

"I'll get some."

He started to say something, but Georgia gave another loud sneeze and the horse jerked sideways. Marty let out a yell of pain and fell back against the side of the stall.

"Are you okay?" She was holding the reins, trying to quiet Sky. Marty hadn't gotten up.

"Damn her silly stupid brains . . ." Slowly he was

boosting himself up, bracing his hands against the side of the stall. He was swearing quietly and steadily.

"Whoa, Sky, whoa, hold on." She moved cautiously around the horse's head to Marty's side of the stall and pushed the horse over. "Marty, are you okay?"

"No, I'm not okay. Get Gran." He was trying to hop out of the stall. Each move made him groan. "She kicked me. Busted my damned leg."

"Oh, no!" She reached him and tried awkwardly to help. "Lean on me."

He put one hand on her shoulder, the other on the front of the stall, and hopped out of range of Sky's hooves. "Get Gran."

Georgia ran for the house. She found Mrs. Ross watching the news on TV. Elmore had just driven up in the pickup, and he stood looking at the screen, his black hat shoved onto the back of his head and a cigar in his hand.

Vera Ross turned to Georgia and said, "Something's happened."

"My horse kicked Marty. He thinks his leg is broken."

Elmore didn't hesitate for a moment. "Call Doc Jaworski," he said to his mother, "and tell him we're on our way." He was out the door and halfway to the stable before Georgia had time to say anything else.

When she came out, Marty was leaning against the side of the stable, and Elmore was backing the pickup toward him.

Elmore lifted Marty into the cab of the truck as easily and gently as if Marty were a small child. Without a word from either of them the pickup drove away, easing carefully over the bumpy places in the driveway.

Vera Ross stood on the back steps. "There goes his motorcycle," she said.

"What?"

"He was saving the money from his job to buy a motorcycle. He won't be driving a tractor for a while."

Georgia felt terrible. "It was my horse."

Mrs. Ross glanced at her. "Well, don't you go feeling guilty. It wasn't you kicked him. Was his idea to get them horses."

"I'll take care of the horses until he's all right."

"I don't suppose they need a whole lot of care. A few of them pellets he gives 'em, some water in the trough. They'll be all right where they are. You better turn Sky out of the stable."

"I will. And I'll work with them every day in the corral, so they won't forget what he's taught them."

Mrs. Ross gave her a sudden smile. "Don't worry so much, child. A boy raises wild horses, he's apt to get hurt. He'll be all right. He's tough, like me."

Georgia backed Sky out of her stall. The little horse obeyed as meekly as if wicked thoughts never crossed her mind. Her dark, liquid eyes regarded Georgia with curiosity, as if to say, "What now?"

"You ought to be ashamed," Georgia said. "You

broke Marty's leg. After all he's done for you."

Sky bent her head toward the pocket in Georgia's denim jacket, looking for the carrot that Georgia sometimes brought her.

"There's nothing there. You don't get rewarded for doing bad things. Back up, back up . . ." She got her out of the stall and led Sky around behind the stable.

She was worried. Maybe they'd have to give up the mustangs, if Marty couldn't work with them.

It was dark, and the evening star looked brilliant in the blue-black sky. The snowy outline of the Sapphire Mountains was faintly visible in the distance. "I suppose you wish you were up there running wild. Why can't you settle down? Act civilized? I can't keep you if you're going to hurt people."

Sky nickered and did a fancy little step sideways.

"I know. You want to be up in the mountains. I hate the mountains. I feel like they're going to fall on me."

Sky rubbed her head against Georgia's arm, and Georgia was seized with a rush of love. "Oh, Sky, please be good. I need you."

She took off the hackamore. "Go have your supper. See you tomorrow." She gave Sky a gentle slap, but the horse stood still, looking at Georgia. "You're not beautiful, Sky, but you're my horse. Go on, join your friends."

This time Sky loped off to join the other three

who were grazing near the pole fence that bounded the property. Georgia looked at their dark shapes. It was strange to find herself falling in love with an ugly little mustang. But that was what was happening.

16

SHE WENT to the Rosses' place every afternoon when she got home from school. By the time she had worked with all four of the horses in the corral and attended to their food and water and now and then brushed them down, she was tired and dirty and the darkness was coming down.

Vera Ross had told her to work for her only on weekends as long as Marty couldn't help with the horses. He was being kept in the hospital for a while with his leg in traction. Georgia went to see him on Sunday afternoon and gave him a full report on the horses. He looked different, lying there in that white bed, with his leg held up at an odd angle by that complicated contraption. He looked lonesome. She wished he could have one of the kittens with him.

He seemed pleased at all she was doing with the horses. "If you want to try a saddle on Sky," he said, "use that old stock saddle that I had when I was a kid. It's a lot lighter than the others and it might not spook her so much."

Georgia wasn't sure she had the courage to try the saddle, but she didn't say so.

Afterward when Vera Ross was driving them home in Elmore's pickup, she pointed to a small house and said, "That's where your buddy Angela lives."

"It is?" Georgia looked at it with interest. "Vera can you let me out? Angela hasn't been to school all week. I better find out what's wrong. I can walk home from here."

When Vera let her out, she walked up to the house. It wasn't till she was nearly at the door that she remembered all that about Angela never asking her to come here. Was it all right to knock on the door? She hesitated. But while she stood there, a little boy, about four years old, came running around the house pretending to ride a horse. He was "giddaping" and "ho, boy"-ing so enthusiastically that he didn't notice Georgia until he was almost upon her. He skidded to a stop and stared at her.

"That's a nice horse you got there," she said.

"He ain't real," the child said.

"He looks real to me."

"He does?" The boy looked down as if to check on it.

"Sure he does. A nice little black stallion with a silver mane. What's his name?"

"Charlie."

[93]

"That's a good name for a horse. Are you Angela's brother?"

"Nah. She's my aunt."

"Oh."

A young woman who looked a little like Angela burst out of the front door calling, "Stevie! Stevie, come finish your milk. You can't just—" She saw Georgia and stopped short. "Hi."

"Hi," Georgia said. "I was looking for Angela. I mean I was wondering if she was sick or something."

"Got the flu."

"Oh. I'm sorry. I'm Georgia."

The young woman nodded. "The kid with the horse."

"Yes." She felt awkward because the sister didn't ask her in. "Can I get anything for Angela?"

"No, she's all right. Just needs to sleep off the fever."

It seemed a casual way to treat the flu. Georgia looked past the sister into the dark hall, hoping to see Angela's mother. There was no one there, but she heard a baby crying. The sister heard it too and shot an anxious glance back at the hall.

"Well," Georgia said, "please tell your mother if she needs any errands run or anything, I'm good at that."

The little boy was standing very close to Georgia looking up at her. He had a runny nose. "She ain't got any mother," he said.

"Get in the house, Stevie," the young woman

said. And to Georgia, "He means my mother died. Last year. I'll tell Angela you was asking." She went inside and closed the door.

Stevie lingered. "You got a horse?" he said.

"Yes." Mother died last year? But hadn't Angela said . . . ? What had she said?

"You can ride Charlie next time you come."

"Thank you, Stevie. I'd like that." She wished she had something to give him. But maybe that would be patronizing. He was a nice little boy. She gave him a Kleenex, and when he looked at it blankly, she took it back and wiped his nose. "Go in and drink your milk now."

"All right." He slapped the flanks of his gleaming black stallion and galloped into the house.

Georgia walked down the road thinking about Angela, wondering how it was possible to be so wrong about people.

At home she changed into her old jeans and went to the Ross place to work with the horses. Weekends were good days because she wasn't so pressured for time. Today she was going to try the little saddle on Sky.

She worked with the other horses first, and then fitted the hackamore onto Sky's nose and led her into the corral. Part of her mind had been thinking about Angela. A song that Aunt Maisie sang sometimes, when she was fooling around with her guitar, kept running through her mind: "Everybody needs somebody that he can talk to." It was a fast, jazzy song, with heavy accent on the two "body" sounds and on "can" and "to." She sang it as she led Sky into the corral and closed the gate. "You like that better than *La Boheme*, huh?"

Sky flicked her ears and craned her neck to see what Georgia was up to.

Georgia latched the gate. It was an old one, not as sturdy as it might be, and it was almost a foot shorter than the corral. She walked Sky out to the snubbing post and started her off first at a trot, then at a lope. She liked the way Sky moved. In spite of that tough little body, there was a grace and control that promised good riding.

Eventually she got the child's saddle and approached Sky. Might as well get it over with. The horse danced playfully away.

"Come on, don't be coy. You aren't going to mind this. I hope."

It took a few minutes to get Sky to stand still. She stroked her and talked to her quietly. "You remind me of Angela sometimes, you know it? You like to stay just out of reach, and you're always ready to take off, quick as a flash. But you can trust me. I like you. I never thought I would. You were a truly horrendous sight the day you came. But you look pretty good now. Just hold still a minute. Like the dentist says, this isn't going to hurt a bit." She draped the stirrups and cinch strap and latigo over the saddle so nothing would hang loose to alarm Sky. Gently she lifted the saddle onto the horse's back.

She felt Sky's muscles tense and twitch, and she took the saddle off quickly before Sky could buck it off. Marty had said that once they buck and get away with it, they'll try it again and again.

In a few minutes she tried the saddle once more, but again she had to take it off fast before Sky could buck. This time Sky started galloping around the corral, around and around and around.

"All right," Georgia said. "That's it for today. You can calm down." She hung the saddle on the fence and when she was able to slow Sky to a stop, she took off the hackamore. "Tomorrow's another day."

In the house she cleaned the kitchen and then joined Vera in a cup of camomile tea. "I'm never going to get a saddle on that horse."

"Sure you will." Vera put down her crossword puzzle. "The way I hear it, patience is the name of the hoss game."

Georgia sighed and said, "I guess," in a discouraged voice.

Vera dumped some sugar into her tea. "Feelin' kind of blue?"

Georgia tried to smile. "When you say 'hoss' like that, it reminds me of home."

"Homesick?"

"I guess in one way. I don't want to go back there, not for anything. But I miss my friends and everything." She took a sip of tea. "I don't want to leave Sky, now that I've got her."

Vera nodded. "I recall when I left Rhode Island. I was eighteen and I thought it was the end of the world. Couldn't imagine what 'out West' would look like."

Georgia tried to imagine Vera at eighteen. She couldn't do it, except for the eyes. They wouldn't be so different. "Did you leave to get married?"

"Yep. But getting married don't mean the world's going to turn into a bowl of cherries. I hardly knew the fella." She chuckled. "Just knew he was handsome. He wore one of those ten-gallon hats."

"How long before you got over being homesick?"

"It kind of wears off. You don't wake up one morning and find out you aren't homesick any more. It comes and goes for a while, like rheumatism. I still get a twinge now and then." She lit a cigarette and blew a thin smoke ring. "I'd like to see a good sailboat race. Lord almighty, wouldn't I like to see a boat race. Like birds, skimming across the bay . . ."

"We were more inland," Georgia said. "But I know what you mean. Boats are pretty."

Vera sighed. "Well, I got no complaints." She looked at the end of her cigarette. "I think I'm going to get me one of those little pipes, like that woman from Jersey, the one that was in congress. I saw her on TV, with a little pipe." She leaned back in her chair, cautiously moving her stiff shoulders. "What do you say to a piece of chocolate pie? It's got enough calories in it to sink a ship, but what do we care? Us and our girlish figures." She gave her little bark of a laugh and got up.

"I'd love a piece." Georgia was trying to think what she missed most. Maybe a polo game. There was a hunt club in her town, and in the summer they played polo on weekends. In her mind she heard the thud of horses' bodies against each other and the whack of wooden mallet on wooden ball. Those horses were so beautiful and so skillful, like the quarterhorses out here that could stop and start and turn on a dime. Poor little Sky.

17

SHE WAITED for Angela after school. Angela hadn't mentioned Georgia's visit, so Georgia didn't speak of it either. Maybe her sister hadn't told her. Angela looked pale and she moved listlessly, unlike her usual quick self. Georgia looked at her with new sympathy, knowing about her mother. If her own mother died, she didn't think she could stand it. She understood why Angela never acknowledged it. "I don't see her much socially myself," she had said, that day. It made Georgia's heart ache for her.

When they got to Georgia's house, her mother met them at the door, smiling. "I've got news!" she called, before they even got to the door.

"What?" For a second Georgia thought she was going to say they were going home, and that her father was never going to lose his temper again. But that wasn't possible.

"I've got you a voice teacher. A good one. She teaches at the music school."

Georgia whooped with joy. She hugged Angela and then hugged her mother. "I can't believe it."

"Saturday mornings at ten."

"But you'll have to drive into Missoula a million times on Saturdays . . ."

"Not a million, honey. Only twice. I'll take you in, and I'll shop or something while you're having your lesson. Then I'll take you home, and I'll still have four hours before I leave for work. No problem."

Georgia hugged her again. It meant her mother's Saturdays would be shot; it was a true gift. But voice lessons! It was almost more than she could believe.

"Now you'll have to try out for the musical evening," Angela said.

Georgia's mother made cocoa for them while Georgia changed into her working clothes. She had not told her mother about Angela's mother; it had seemed too awful to talk about, somehow. Now she wished she had, in case her mother should ask about her. But when she came into the kitchen, they were sitting with their heads together, looking at pictures of tennis players in *Newsweek* magazine. It struck Georgia that they looked more like mother and daughter than she and her mother did. How could that be? Physically they were quite different. But it was something about their expressions, and maybe that they were interested in the same things.

"I didn't know you liked tennis," she said to Angela.

"I play some," Angela said matter-of-factly. "Don't have much chance to practice."

"I'm terrible at tennis. I'm so bad, my father says it doesn't make any difference which end of the racket I hold."

Her mother got up. "I've got to get dressed for work. Is Angela going to watch you work with the horses?"

"She doesn't like horses."

Angela said nothing. Georgia's mother glanced at her and said, "I bet she'd like to watch you, though."

"Sure," Angela said with a shrug. "Why not?"

Georgia felt her mother's eyes sternly upon her so she tried not to show her annoyance, but really, she did wish Mom would mind her own business. She did not, definitely did not, want anybody watching her. Except, of course, Marty, who would be home from the hospital soon. He would watch and tell her what she was doing wrong, and that was okay because he knew. Well, she was stuck with Angela now, like it or not.

When they were on their way to the Ross place, Angela pushing her bike, Angela said, "You don't have to ask me if you don't want to. I mean, I don't care one way or the other."

Georgia glanced at her. Angela's face looked thin, almost pinched. Georgia remembered then how it felt when you were getting over the flu. You were weak and tired and depressed. "Sure I want you," she said. "I just thought you don't like horses."

"I don't mind looking at them."

"Right. Fine. You can meet Vera. You'll like her."

But Vera was taking a nap when they got there, so they went directly to the corral. Angela sat on the top pole of the fence, balancing precariously, while Georgia went to get the little black stallion.

But the stallion was not in the mood to be caught. She gave up after a few minutes and brought Sky back instead. "This is my horse," she told Angela. "Isn't she ugly?"

"I think she's cute."

"Hear that?" Georgia said to Sky. "She thinks you're cute." She slipped the hackamore over her muzzle and adjusted it. "So show her how smart you are."

Sky was in a cooperative mood. Georgia guided her around the corral for about twenty minutes, glancing toward Angela now and then. She expected her friend to get bored and leave, but Angela sat very still, watching.

Georgia got the saddle. She didn't like doing this with someone watching, but she was anxious to get Sky broken to the saddle before Marty saw her.

Sky was eating some brown grass as Georgia

came up to her. She looked around curiously. Georgia talked to her and stroked her for a minute, and then she laid the saddle on her back, prepared to duck. Nothing happened. Sky looked at her and went back to cropping the dry grass.

Shaking with excitement, Georgia gently pulled her up and led her around the corral. She kept waiting for Sky to buck, but the little horse behaved as if a saddle were a part of her daily experience. She was so calm, Georgia decided to try tightening the cinch. Sky peered at her to see what she was doing, but she made no objection. After a few minutes Georgia loosened the cinch and took off the saddle. No use pushing her luck.

She worked for a little while with the other horses, and all the time Angela sat quietly on the fence. Georgia had never seen her still for so long.

When they walked back to Georgia's house, Angela said, "That's a skill."

"What is?"

"Working like that with horses."

"Oh." Georgia didn't know what to say, but she was pleased.

When they got to the house, her mother had already left for work. She looked at Angela, who was getting ready to mount her bike and take off. "You want to stay for supper? My mother left me some real good beef stroganoff."

"What's that?"

"Well, you take little pieces of beef and tomato

paste and sour cream and a bunch of stuff . . . It's good."

"Do you eat supper by yourself?"

"Sure."

"All right." Angela put her bike down. "I'll stay."

She called her sister and then watched the six o'clock news while Georgia took a shower and got into clean clothes. For a minute Georgia forgot she was there, and she began to sing in the shower as she always did. Then she remembered, but she kept on singing anyway. Maybe Angela would be too busy with the news to listen.

Angela tried the stroganoff cautiously. "Oh," she said. "Hey, that's good."

"My mom is a terrific cook. The man where she works says he might use her for substitute cook when his regular goes on vacation."

"I heard you singing in the shower."

"Oh. I always do that. I guess people do."

"I don't."

"Well, a lot of people do. The acoustics are good. You sound better than you are."

Angela drank some milk. It left a thin white moustache on her upper lip. "You and your mother are real smart people."

"Mom is." Georgia felt embarrassed but pleased. Connie had never said she was smart. She was the one who thought Connie was smart.

"My mother is dead," Angela said.

It was unexpected. Georgia choked a little on her baked potato. "I'm sorry. I don't know how you stand that."

"Oh, well." Angela's voice changed. It was almost gay. "Here today, gone tomorrow. Can I have some more of that stuff? What makes it pink?"

"Tomato paste." Georgia got up to refill Angela's plate. "My father's got a terrible temper. He beat up my mother."

"Mine's in prison." She gave Georgia a dazzling smile. "We sure know how to pick 'em, don't we?"

"Yeah. We do." It was the first night since her mother had gone to work that she had eaten her supper without feeling like dying of loneliness. "We've got chocolate eclairs for dessert."

18

ANGELA WENT to the Ross place again with Georgia the next day. While she was helping Georgia with the pellets and the watering trough, Marty came out to the stable on crutches.

"Hey," he said, "how's the hired help?" He had a wide grin, but he looked pale after his stay in the hospital.

"Marty! It's great you're back." Georgia introduced him to Angela.

"The horses look good, much as I can see of 'em. Did you put that glue on Sky's hoofs?"

"No, I was going to but . . ."

"But you forgot."

"No, honest, I didn't. I couldn't get her to stand still so I could get at her."

"Get your buddy here to help."

"She's . . . she doesn't like horses much . . ."

"I'm scared of 'em," Angela said. "I get asthma."

"Well, we can't have you gettin' asthma. Tell you what, Georgia, you bring Sky up here, and I'll talk to her while you glue her up. You got the glue here?"

"Yes. But what if you got hurt again?"

"You know what they say, if you almost drown, go back in the water." He winked at Angela. "Go get her, George."

When Georgia brought Sky back to the stable, Angela and Marty were chatting like old friends.

"I can help," Angela said. "Where's the glue?"

"On the shelf." Georgia pointed.

"I can be a big help," Angela said, her eyes dancing. "I can take the top off the glue." She got it and handed it to Georgia, keeping well out of range of Sky.

Bracing himself on his crutches and resting the heel of his cast on the floor, Marty began talking to Sky and rubbing her nose. "You look good, old friend. Your partner's been taking good care of you. You look almost civilized, yes, you do."

Georgia hunkered down by the horse's back hoof and dipped the applicator into the glue. Very carefully she painted the whole hoof. Then she moved to the other side and did the other one. She was nervous when she got to the front feet. Sky could see her and was tensing a little. Marty soothed her and stroked her. In the same tone of voice he said, "Hurry up,

George, don't take all day. This baby's gettin' just a little bit antsy."

Georgia finished the front feet and stepped back. "It's done."

"Good girl. Both of you. You too Angela, over there in the far corner. You breathin' okay?"

"Yeah," Angela said. "I think I'll go outside now."

Georgia backed Sky out of the stall, led her outside, and let her go. "You smell terrible with that icky glue," she said. She gave her a gentle slap, and Sky galloped away, toward the clump of birch trees in the far corner of the pasture.

Suddenly Marty said, "Oh no!" and began to laugh.

"What?"

"She's going to get leaves stuck all over her feet."

"Sky!" Georgia ran to get her, but by the time she got there, there were clumps of yellow leaves stuck to Sky's hooves. Georgia had trouble getting her away from that part of the pasture, and it was too late to get the leaves unstuck. Marty and Angela were doubled up with laughter as Georgia led her horse to the corral, Sky walking in a gingerly way as if she couldn't figure out what had happened.

"She's got her clown costume on," Angela said. "I think she looks beautiful."

"Poor Sky." Georgia put her arm around the horse's neck. "They'll come off sooner or later. Don't feel bad." And to Marty and Angela she said, "I don't think it's nice to laugh at her." But when she looked at Sky's feet, she had to laugh, too.

"She looks as if she could fly," Angela said. "They look like feathers."

"She could fly if she wanted to," Georgia said. She kissed Sky's nose. "Sky can do anything."

"I got to get off these crutches," Marty said. "Come on up to the house, and Gran will make us some tea."

"Pegasus," Vera said, when they called her out on the back steps to look at Sky. "That's who she is, Pegasus. I'm glad to see you, Angela. You like devil's-food cake?"

"Sure," Angela said. She gave Vera her widest smile.

"Well, come in then. Don't stand around in the cold."

19

GEORGIA LED SKY down the road toward the mountains. The horse had grown used to the saddle now, but Georgia still had not tried to ride her. Marty had said, "Give it another week." The idea was to do everything gradually, so Sky never got spooked.

Georgia was listening to the Walkman that her mother had bought her. A woman announcer was reading off community activities. Georgia repeated them aloud to Sky. "Listen to this one: 'Dating Hints, followed by a social evening for teens and their parents.' And their parents? Would you want your parents around while you talked about what to do on a date?"

On a day like this, Jerry would be on the football field. Connie had owed her a letter for quite a while. Out of sight, out of mind.

Sky swished her tail at a grasshopper that had

lighted on her back. Georgia brushed the insect off and felt the tremor of irritation in Sky's muscles. "It was only a grasshopper. Don't let it bug you." She giggled. "Bug you, get it?"

A few minutes later she laughed again at the voice on the radio. "Oh no! The Valley Chicken-Slappers are holding a square dance. Chicken-Slappers...I don't believe it. I'll have to write Connie about that. This is a funny place, Sky. I can't get used to it." She shut off the radio. "Would you like Massachusetts? There are horses all over the place. Only they'd turn up their noses at you. They're snobbish horses." She put her arm around Sky's neck. "I wouldn't take ten of them for you."

They crossed a field and came out on a dirt road. "Two weeks from today," Georgia said, "the Met season on the radio starts. And I begin voice lessons." It scared her and made her happy at the same time. Her teacher at home hadn't been all that great, but this one was supposed to be good. She taught at the university and that was where Judith Blegen had gone. What if the teacher thought Georgia wasn't any good? What if she really *wasn't* any good? That thought was always in her mind. Just because her grandmother sang in opera didn't mean *she* was good.

She heard the sound of a car, and she led Sky up a slight rise into a field, to wait for the car to go by. Sky watched nervously as the noisy little VW came into view and drove on. Georgia talked to her soothingly. "It's just a little VW Bug. Hey, we got bugs on the brain today. Don't be scared, it won't climb up here. Look, there's a bunch of your mountains over there. Not *your* mountains really, but something like them, I suppose." She shaded her eyes and gazed at the rugged mountains. She could see horses grazing at the top of one of them where there were no trees. It must get mighty cold up there. And you wouldn't think they could find all that much to eat, but Marty said they could.

Sky lifted her head and seemed also to be looking in the direction of the range. She stood very still, as if listening.

Georgia said, "What do you hear?"

To their left there was a chain link fence topped with barbed wire that enclosed part of the small ranch adjoining the Ross place.

"They must not have any horses," Georgia said. "Or they wouldn't have barbed wire. A horse could get hurt." A moment later she pointed. "Cows." There were half a dozen black Angus grazing in the field.

The wind off the mountains was cold. There was a feeling of snow in the air. "I can smell snow," she said.

Tomorrow was Thanksgiving. Her mother had to work, but they were having a turkey dinner at one o'clock, and her mother had let her invite Angela. Afterwards they were going to the Rosses' to have some of Vera's plum pudding. It sounded like a good day. At home Aunt Maisie would be cooking a goose for all the relatives, including Marge.

She leaned down and pulled off one of the torn and trampled leaves that still stuck to Sky's hooves. "So I'm not there. Big deal. If I were there, I wouldn't have you. Or Angela or the Rosses. And Mom wouldn't have learned how to make such good huevos rancheros. Come on, let's go home. I'm freezing."

Sky resisted for a minute, and Georgia tugged at the hackamore impatiently. Sky planted her feet and hunched her back muscles.

Georgia let up on the reins. "Oh, no, oh, no, I'm sorry, don't buck. I know, you hate to be pushed. I'm sorry." She waited a minute and then gently urged the horse toward the road. But Sky had decided to munch on a tuft of frost-blackened grass. Georgia waited. "I don't know sometimes," she said, "who's breaking who."

20

I RODE SKY ! ! ! !

Georgia printed the words in capital letters under the heading of "Thanksgiving Night, three minutes till midnight."

She was sitting on her bed with the three kittens curled up around her. Although she had said several times during this long day that she could not eat another bite of anything, she was eating a small wedge of her mother's squash pie. Angela had never heard of squash pie, and it turned out that the Rosses hadn't either, except for Vera. "Yankee pie," Elmore had said. "Must be Yankee pie." Elmore and Angela had taken a liking to each other, and Elmore had talked more than Georgia had ever heard him.

She and Angela and her mother had had a good time and a very good dinner. A big turkey; mashed potatoes with a little cream and lots of butter, the way

Georgia liked them; parsnips, which Georgia didn't like; and Harvard beets, which she did; green peas that her mom had frozen in September when they first came; cranberries with orange peel; her mother's super chestnut stuffing. And squash pie with sharp cheddar cheese from Vermont, which Aunt Maisie had sent. They really stuffed themselves.

But long before the dinner, Angela had arrived dragging some fence posts, and the two of them had worked all morning to finish up the corral. Because tomorrow was the best day: Sky was coming home.

Today had been the first best day, when Marty had said in the afternoon, "It's time you got on that horse's back. She ain't any good walking around like a dog on a leash."

She was excited and scared. Before he took her out to the corral, he admitted he had gotten on her himself that morning, and she hadn't made a fuss. "Don't stay on more than a minute or so, and if you feel her start to tense up, get off quick. We don't want her to get the notion she can buck you off."

Angela had clung to the fence, her arms wound through the poles, her fingers crossed. Vera and El-more had come down to watch, too, but Marty wouldn't let them come close because he didn't want Sky distracted.

His leg encased in the heavy cast, he used a crutch like a cane when he walked on the uneven ground of the corral and the pasture. But now he gave the crutch to Angela to hold for him and hobbled over to the snubbing post, where Georgia was talking to Sky. She put the saddle on and tightened the cinch. Sky looked bored.

Both of them talked to Sky for a few minutes. Marty had his hand on the hackamore close to her muzzle, holding it easily. He gave Georgia a nod. She took the reins in her hand and put her left foot in the stirrup. Stirrups were a lot longer with a western saddle, she thought; that ought to help. She held her breath and swung her leg over the saddle. She was up. Sky looked around at her, and then went back to poking at Marty's pockets in search of a lump of sugar or a carrot.

Georgia felt as though she were sitting on top of the world. She was sitting on her own horse! It was a dark, storm-threatening day, with a chilly wind, but she felt as warm as if she were sitting in bright sunlight.

"Okay," Marty said. "That's enough for today."

Angela and Vera and even Elmore congratulated her as if she had done something wonderful. It was Sky they ought to congratulate, she thought. Sweet Sky.

Later, when they were eating Vera's plum pudding, Marty said that Georgia could take Sky over to her place the next day.

"Is your place fenced in the back?" Elmore asked her.

"It wasn't all the way until this morning. Angela finished it. It's real secure now."

Angela grinned and tossed her braid. "Just stuck in a few old posts is all. Nothing to it."

"Nothing but hard work," Elmore said. "If it wasn't for the boy here, I wouldn't bother with horses none at all. There's always something you got to be doing for 'em."

"Next winter you can graze Sky up on the mountain," Marty said. He grinned at the indignant look Georgia gave him.

"I might as well have left her in the Pryor Mountains as do that," Georgia said. "I want her close by, where I can look after her."

"You can't baby a wild mustang."

"She isn't wild any more."

"Don't tease the child," Vera said to Marty. "Angela, you have yourself some more puddin'. No use having it hanging around."

Angela had more pudding.

That night Georgia was too excited to sleep. She shifted Pang off her stomach and unwound Pong from her neck. Ping was asleep at the foot of the bed. She thought about Cinders and hoped Jill had given him some turkey gizzard. He loved it. Cats had funny tastes. Pong loved uncooked spaghetti, and he would go around with a long piece hanging out of his mouth like a cigarette.

She yawned again and thought how good it had felt to be up on Sky at last. Her own horse, forever.

She hoped Angela had had a good time. She

thought of Stevie and his horse Charlie. She'd like to get Stevie a Christmas present.

She had promised Angela she would try out for the musical evening on Monday. She really didn't want to. It would be hard to get up and sing in front of all those kids whom she still didn't know very well. She thought she might do "Silent Night" in German, like the Schumann-Heinke record her dad had played every Christmas since she could remember. Would the kids here think she was showing off if she sang it in German?

21

GEORGIA WANTED to ride Sky over to her new home, but Marty thought that was pushing her luck. "Don't make her get adjusted to too many things at once."

Georgia agreed, because Marty knew a lot more about horses than she did, but she was secretly glad that from now on Sky would be entirely her horse, and she would get to make the decisions.

Angela was baby-sitting her nieces and nephews, so only Georgia's mother was there to witness the triumphal procession. She stood on the porch, watching Georgia and Sky come up the road. It was a slow business, because Sky liked to stop often to investigate things along the side of the road.

"You're worse than a puppy," Georgia told her.

At the house she stopped so her mother could get a good look at the new member of the family. Her mother was not a horsewoman. She had a strange expression on her face as she got her first close-up look at the mustang.

"Isn't she a sweetheart?" Georgia said.

"I'm sure she's very nice," her mother said, pulling back a little as Sky turned curiously toward her.

Georgia was hurt. Why couldn't her mother see what a wonderful horse Sky was? All right, she had been shocked the first time she saw her, but that was before Sky had been cleaned up and groomed and tamed. Georgia turned away, feeling disappointed and a little indignant. Her mother ought to be a better judge of character than that.

She took Sky into the barn and showed her the stall, cleaned out and swept. She had bought her own set of currycomb and brushes. Vera had figured out that with the twenty-five dollars Georgia's mother had contributed and the weeks Georgia had worked, she had paid for her horse. Now she got paid in cash.

When she had shown Sky the barn, she took her out and showed her the corral and then the newly fenced pasture. "Angela did most of this for you. The old fence was falling down. She can't get close to you because she gets asthma, but she's your friend." She took off the halter and stood for a few minutes watching Sky investigate her new quarters. When the little horse had settled down to chewing the last leaves off a chokecherry bush, Georgia started back toward the house, but as she reached the gate, Ping and Pang raced past her into the pasture, straight toward Sky.

"Oh, no! Ping! Pang! Here, kitty, kitty..." Georgia tried to circle around them, knowing that if she chased them, they'd run all the faster. But they were way ahead of her.

They dashed up to Sky and tumbled over her front hooves as if she were another, larger kitten. Georgia held her breath and prayed. Sky lifted one foot and then bent her head to see what these little creatures were. She didn't seem alarmed. But Ping was now rolling around in the place where Sky would certainly put down her heavy hoof. If Georgia ran for them, she would startle Sky. And anyway there wasn't time to reach her.

Very carefully Sky put down her hoof where it wouldn't touch the kitten and stepped one step back. Georgia let out her breath. "Oh, thanks, God. She knows enough not to hurt them. Oh, no kidding, thanks an awful lot."

As soon as she safely could, she reached the kittens, scooped them up, and took them in the house. Then she went back to the corral and put her arm around Sky's neck. "What a good horse! I can trust you. You and I are going to be friends forever." She kissed Sky's nose. The horse shook herself and leaned down to bite off a mouthful of dry brown grass. Georgia laughed. "So you're not sentimental. But you love me, I know you do."

22

GEORGIA WOKE UP, hearing the phone ring. By the time she made herself get up and wander sleepily downstairs to answer it, her mother had come in from work and was talking. Georgia listened for a moment and knew it was her father on the other end. She felt a lurch of worry as she always did when he called or a letter came from him. She knew things were hard for her mother, and Georgia couldn't help being afraid that she would give in and go back to him. After all, she had been in love with him once.

She went back to bed. Her mother came in a little later.

"Your father has a new job."

"That's good. Maybe he'll send you some money."

"No. As long as I stay here, I'll do it on my own."

As long as I stay here. The phrase hung in Georgia's mind, troubling her long after her mother had said good night. You couldn't put a horse in a van and take him across the United States. And she wouldn't go without Sky. If it came right down to it, she would run away.

ON SATURDAY AFTERNOON when Angela came over, Georgia was in the barn currying Sky and listening to *Madama Butterfly* on the Metropolitan Opera Broadcast. The music from the small portable radio filled the barn.

"Where's your Walkman?" Angela said, without bothering with hi.

"In the house."

"What's that you're listening to? Hi, Sky."

"*Madama Butterfly*." Georgia straightened up. "I didn't get to take my lesson. My teacher has the flu."

"Oh, rotten luck. Well, you can practice for the tryout. Who's that singing?"

"I'm not sure. She's playing Suzuki."

"Come on. Suzuki is a car."

"Not this one. Stand still, Sky."

"What are they singing about? What's the story?"

Georgia wished Angela would hush so she could listen to the music. "Oh, this Japanese girl marries an American Navy guy, and she has a baby and he ditches her, so she kills herself."

Angela thought about it. "I wouldn't kill myself for some guy."

"Me either," Georgia said emphatically.

"How old is she?"

"Fifteen."

Angela looked shocked. "Fifteen! That poor little kid. Did she shoot herself?"

"No. She used a sword." Georgia turned Sky's head toward her and combed her mane.

"A sword! That would hurt!"

"Naturally." She wanted to listen to "Un Bel Di." How come Angela always talked when a person wished she'd be quiet?

But surprisingly Angela did stay silent all through the aria. "That's very sad," she said at the end of it. "I guess someday you'll sing that in some big opera house, huh?"

Georgia laughed, but her impatience evaporated. Angela believed in her! Come to think of it, she didn't know anybody else who did. Her father certainly had his doubts, and her mother acted as if Georgia taking singing lessons was like Marge when she took piano lessons, something you did to make you better educated. But Angela could see her, as Georgia saw herself, standing on a stage singing Butterfly! She was touched.

"Come on in and I'll make some cocoa," she said.

In the house Angela sipped her cocoa thoughtfully. "I'm almost fifteen," she said. "Like that Japanese kid. Maybe we're not so bad off as we think we are, Georgia."

"Some days," Georgia said, "I don't feel bad off at all." Today was one of them. She had Sky. She had Angela for a friend. She had the Rosses. "I guess I'll try out for the concert."

"Good." Angela dumped some more sugar into her cocoa. "You'll knock 'em dead."

23

THE TIME HAD COME to take Sky out for a real ride. The weather was chilly, and there was a sharp wind coming down from Canada, the weatherman said. The sky looked like lead, and as Georgia and Sky started down the road, she couldn't see the tops of the mountains. It had been densely foggy for a couple of days, but the wind was sweeping that murky gray stuff away.

Sky was feeling frisky. Georgia thought of that song, "Don't Fence Me In." It had been written by a Montanan, and that figured. This was the land of space. "So you don't like to be fenced in," Georgia said to Sky. "All right, here we go."

Sky flicked her ears, and at a touch of Georgia's heels she broke into a fast trot. There was no way you could post on Sky, the way you did on eastern horses. All you could do was settle in to the mustang's hard but regular rhythm. It wasn't a rocking-chair gait, like some of the riding school horses at home; it was more strenuous, but also more exciting.

She glanced at the clouds and wondered if it was going to snow. Further north it was snowing hard, the radio had said, and there was a travel advisory. She knew her mother worried about not being able to get to work when the snows came. But today she herself didn't feel like worrying about anything.

She had tried out for the school concert and been accepted. She was pleased and a little scared. But she didn't want to think about that now. She turned Sky's head toward the wide field beyond the farm where the black Angus were, heading toward the foothills.

Sky broke into a gallop. The wind took Georgia's breath away. She tucked her chin inside her scarf and hunkered down in the saddle. Sky's hooves pounded on the frozen earth. Georgia relaxed into the rhythm, almost welcoming the regular jolt. She became part of the motion, horse and girl moving together like one creature. Never had she felt so exhilarated. She wanted to yell with delight, but the wind snatched her voice away.

On across the field Sky galloped, never slackening pace. Georgia let her have her head. As they came toward a line of trees, Sky veered to the right, onto a dirt road, on down the road till there was a clear field that sloped up toward the mountains.

Georgia's eyes and nose were streaming and her hair had whipped out from under her wool cap, blowing across her face. She felt totally happy, and more alive than she had known anyone could be.

Finally Sky slowed down, as the land rose upward. She was heading for the mountains. Georgia got her breath, wiped her face, and said, "Wow!" in a faint voice that was all she had left at the moment. "Sky!" she said. She leaned forward for a moment, her arms along the muscular neck.

They found a jeep trail. In a little while they came to a stream, not very wide, but wide enough for a wooden bridge. As Sky hesitated, Georgia guided her onto the bridge. "Probably this is a fire trail," she said. "Forest Service guys."

Sky stopped short. Georgia urged her on, but she planted her feet and would not move.

"You're being silly," Georgia said. "It's only a bridge." Marty had told her that sometimes horses balked at bridges. "You've got to learn. This looks solid enough, and you'll be across it in a minute."

But Sky refused.

Georgia didn't want to turn back. All this time she had avoided even thinking much about the mountains, but today she felt challenged by them. She wanted to get closer. "They're your kind of place," she told Sky. "All you have to do is get up your nerve and cross that little dinky bridge."

But Sky backed off the bridge altogether. Even that much contact between horse and bridge made the wooden planks rumble. Georgia could see how it might be alarming to a horse. One thing a horse was careful about was where he put his feet. She remembered how careful Sky had been about the kitten.

"All right, you want to go across the stream? You'll get your feet wet." She neck-reined Sky to the left.

Unexpectedly Sky reared, and Georgia found herself on the hard ground, sliding down the bank toward the water. Sky serenely grazed a few yards away.

"Did you *have* to do that? I was trying to be cooperative." She picked herself up and remounted the horse. "Now are you going across that stream or not? I'm supposed to make some decisions around here, you know. And I'm meeting you halfway."

Sky splashed through the water without hesitation, and on the other side they climbed a steep bank into a grove of pines and western larch. Here they were somewhat protected from the wind, although the lowering darkness increased.

Surefooted, Sky picked her way around trees and through thickets until they came to a narrow rising stretch of open land that went up sharply into the base of the mountain. Georgia felt the quickening in Sky's attention. This seemed like home to her.

"You climb like a goat," Georgia said. By this time she was beginning to feel the oppressiveness of the mountain looming so close above her. But she would let Sky go a little further.

The trees thickened, and it was hard to see where they were going, but Sky never hesitated. For the first time Georgia found it possible to imagine her horse living in the Pryor Mountains. Maybe it was wrong to catch those horses and civilize them. Ranchers complained that the horses overgrazed the land, but the horses had been in that country longer than the ranchers had. Not this generation of horses, but their ancestors.

"But if I took you back there," Georgia said, "they'd only round you up again. And a lot of those wild horses are just killed." She shuddered at the thought of this compact bundle of energy ever being dead.

It seemed to be getting suddenly much colder, and a few hard pellets, half snow, half hail, struck her face. "We have to be getting back."

Sky ignored her signals, and Georgia began to feel alarmed. What if she couldn't make Sky go back? What if they went right on to the wild part of these mountains, and she was lost forever?

"That's silly," she told herself. "If you really couldn't get her to turn around, you'd just get off and walk home." She shivered, thinking of it. Anyway she couldn't leave Sky. "Sky! Turn around!" She jerked the reins.

It was definitely snowing now and hard to see more than a couple of feet ahead. Georgia's face ached with cold, and her hands and feet were getting numb. She felt like crying, but when did that ever accomplish anything? "Sky! Turn!"

She was so surprised when Sky did turn, she almost lost her balance. Now Sky moved confidently down the hill as if it were her own idea. Georgia felt weak with relief.

By the time they were back on the dirt road, the snow was driving into their faces and the wind was pounding at them. Georgia felt disoriented. She thought they were headed in the right direction, but she wasn't sure. She tried to guide Sky to the right at the place where she thought the second field was, but Sky ignored her.

"All right, if you know so much, take us home." She felt helpless and scared, but there didn't seem much that she could do except leave it to Sky.

The fields were snow-covered and slippery, but Sky took them at a sure, steady trot, never making any attempt to break into a lope. She seemed to know exactly what she was doing.

Georgia could hardly believe it when they came out on their own road, just above the cattle ranch. A clump of black Angus hung their heads against the snow, huddled together by the barbed wire fence. They looked up with only the faintest curiosity as Sky and Georgia rode by.

When they were safely in the barn, Georgia fed and watered Sky and covered her with the old horse blanket Marty had given her. Her hands and feet tingled painfully as she moved around.

"You were wonderful." She leaned her forehead against Sky's. "Thank you very much. Now I know what horse sense is."

Sky grabbed a mouthful of oats and looked at Georgia as she chewed.

"That was the most wonderful ride I ever had. Now I know I'm alive."

24

GEORGIA RUBBED down Sky, fed her some pellets, and put her out in the pasture. It was taken for granted now that, except on nights when Angela baby-sat for her sister, she would have supper with Georgia and they would do their homework together. Her sister, concerned about Angela's being a burden, often sent a roasted chicken or a pie, a loaf of bread or onions and potatoes from her garden.

Tonight Angela brought two wild ducks that her brother-in-law had shot. They were already roasted and they looked good, although Georgia did not like the idea of eating ducks. People shouldn't shoot them.

A couple of times she and her mother had driven out to the wild bird sanctuary on the road to Stevensville; they had parked and watched the ducks and the other birds.

As if reading her mind, Angela said, "I wish he wouldn't go hunting, but he says if he didn't, we'd run out of meat before the winter's over. Personally I wouldn't care if we did."

Georgia fixed up some poultry dressing mix and put it in the oven along with the baked potatoes. She was washing lettuce when she heard a sound like thunder go by the house. But it was not thunder. She ran for the door and saw Sky galloping down the road toward the mountains.

"Oh, no! Sky got out." She ran out of the house and down the road, but Sky was already way ahead of her. It was her own fault! She should never have let Sky get near those mountains.

She was running so fast that by the time she reached the Ross place, she had a stitch in her side. Marty came out of the yard riding the black stallion.

"Stay here," he yelled at her. "I'll get her." He had a rope coiled around the saddle horn, and he didn't slow down for an answer.

Georgia stood in the middle of the road, panting, watching him tear down the road after Sky. The little stallion was going like the wind.

Angela caught up with her, and they walked in to the Ross house. Elmore was standing on the porch railing, his back braced against the support, looking at the road through binoculars. Vera was rocking nervously in her battered old rocking chair. She lit a cigarette.

"Can you see them?" Georgia asked Elmore.

He jumped down and lifted Georgia up to the rail and handed her the glasses. Every now and then when they came to an open place in the road, she could see Marty and the stallion. She couldn't see Sky.

"That little black feller can really run," Elmore said. "You'd never think it to look at him."

"What if Marty hurts his leg again?" Georgia was worried. He had been out of the cast only a few days.

"Legs don't break chronic," Vera said. "Doctor said he was good as new."

Elmore went into the house and got a can of Budweiser from the refrigerator.

Marty was out of sight now. Georgia jumped down.

Angela touched her arm. "You stay here till Sky comes back, why don't you. I'll take the potatoes out and all that."

Georgia found it hard to think about potatoes. "You go ahead and eat. I'm not hungry."

Angela gave them all her funny little wave that was half a salute and loped off down the driveway.

"That's a good kid," Vera said. She threw her half-smoked cigarette in a glowing arc over the rail and stood up with a sigh. "I got to feed Elmore. You want a little something to hold you together?"

Georgia shook her head. She was staring off in the direction of the mountains. Sky would head for the mountains, she was sure. If she was going at her best speed, Marty didn't have a prayer of catching up with her. Once she got up into the hills, they all might as well forget it.

No, I won't forget it, Georgia said to herself. I'll go up there every day and look for her till I find her. No matter how high up I have to go and how scared I get. She thought about the empty pasture at home, the empty stall in the stable, and tears stung her eyes. She could not, would not, do without Sky. She'd skip school if she had to and search every day.

She walked out to the road and tried to see in the gathering darkness. It seemed to get dark much faster and more suddenly out here. At home there were long twilights. She sat down on a boulder that marked the entrance to the Ross place. What if Marty broke his leg again? He shouldn't be racing around up there in the dark, in those dangerous mountains. If he hadn't found Sky by now, he ought to come back.

She considered riding one of the other horses bareback and going after them, but she had never seen Marty ride either of them. Maybe he hadn't gone that far in training those two. He'd be mad if she messed up his program or if another horse ran away. She decided to walk up the road, too tense to sit still.

When she had gone a short way, she heard horses. It was almost more of a vibration than a sound. She broke into a run.

They were coming at a fast trot, Marty leading

Sky by a rope. He drooped in the saddle as if he were tired. As soon as he saw her, he stopped the horses and handed the rope to Georgia.

"Teach her some manners."

"I'm sorry, Marty. Thanks an awful lot." She wanted to hug Sky, but it didn't seem to be the right moment for that.

"She must have jumped the fence. You better get Angela to take a look."

She wanted to say she could take a look herself, but she didn't. And her second thought was that he was right; Angela could fix a fence a lot better than she could. She was so happy to see Sky, she could hardly think straight.

"Looks like this baby's a jumper."

"I really do thank you."

"I know you do, kid. See you." He touched the black with his boot heels, and they took off.

Georgia led Sky home. The top rail of the gate was hanging by its hinges, where Sky's hooves had struck it as she jumped. The gate was lower than the rest of the fence by about a foot; that was the problem.

Angela came out. "We'll need to make that gate flush with the fence."

"Right. I'll leave her in the stable for now."

Sky followed Georgia meekly and stood while Georgia tied her up in the stall. Georgia felt light-headed with relief that nothing terrible had happened. "Tomorrow," she said, "we'll get that gate so high you can't jump it. That was a bad thing to do, Sky."

She got a bucket of water. The mustang drank thirstily. "Nobody would bring you fresh water and pellets up on the mountain. If you want to be taken good care of, you have to do your part." But what she heard herself saying didn't reassure her. She knew that Sky was not at all concerned with being taken care of. She wanted to be free. "I don't know if there's any such thing as *absolutely* free. You know what happened to you in the Pryors. Here you're loved. Nobody'll hurt you." She leaned against Sky's flank, smelling the dust in her coat. "Maybe we're not like the others, you and me. Kind of misfits or something. But we can't go back where we came from. We've got each other though. That's what counts. And we've got friends, like Angela and the Rosses. Look how Marty came after you. Angela and the Rosses are kind of misfittish too, but that's why we all like each other, right?"

Sky stomped her feet.

"We'll go on trips to the mountains as often as we can. It scares me up there, but I know that's where you want to be. But you have to do your part. Get out of my pocket; there's no sugar in there, just a pencil." She pulled the horse's head up so she could look into her eyes. "Is it a deal? I'll see you tomorrow, but now you're stuck in here because you jumped the gate. Consequences, see? That's what happens."

When she got to the house, the ducks and the potatoes and the salad were on the table. And she discovered that she was hungry after all.

25

ANGELA'S BIG, bearded brother-in-law brought her and a gate to Georgia's house the next afternoon. Georgia was late getting home because she had stayed to practice her carol with the visiting music teacher who was going to accompany her on the piano. It had gone well, and the teacher had told her she had a lovely voice.

She heard the hammering before she got to the house. The pickup was backed up to the fence, and Marvin was holding the gate in place while Angela screwed in the hinges. It wasn't a new gate, but it was a dandy; a little higher than the fence itself, and strong-looking. Sky wouldn't knock that over in a hurry; and if she could jump it, she could jump anything.

They didn't notice her at first, and she stood watching them. She was thinking that none of her neighbors at home would have done a thing like this. Not that they weren't nice, but it just wouldn't occur to them. At home you looked in the Yellow Pages and called a carpenter or whatever.

Marvin saw her and called out, "Hi," in a deep bass voice. She went up to them.

"This is real nice," she said.

"Ought to do the trick. Angie, you're gettin' that screw in crooked. Put your weight under this thing and let me have a go at it."

When it was finished to his satisfaction, he said, "If your mustang jumps this one, she's a champ."

"Gosh, I really do thank you." Remembering her manners she said, "Would you like a cup of coffee or something?"

He smiled at her. "No, thanks. Got to get back to work." He gave the screwdriver back to Angela. "See ya."

"He's nice," Georgia said, as he drove off.

"He's all right."

Georgia brought Sky out and turned her loose in the pasture. She watched anxiously as Sky tore around at top speed. "You don't think she would jump the fence, do you?"

"Who knows what a horse will do?"

As Sky came to a skidding stop at the west end of the pasture, almost crashing into the fence, Georgia said, "The two worrisome places are right there where she is now and down at the east end. If she wanted to bad enough, she could get up speed to maybe clear the fence. On the west she'd be heading for the highway; and at the other end, she'd be able to cut behind the Ross fence, but then she'd be stuck with that barbed wire fence the cow people have."

"Stop worrying," Angela said. "Either we build a fence that reaches to the sky or . . ." She grinned. ". . . or Sky's going to jump over the sky. Like the cow that jumped over the moon. You can't baby-sit her all the time."

"I know. But I worry."

"You are a worrywart."

A little later, as they sat in Georgia's kitchen doing homework, Georgia said, "Speaking of worrying. My father called again last night and talked to my mother, after she got home from work."

"So?"

"So I worry. What if he talked her into going home?"

Angela frowned. "Now you got me worried. She wouldn't do that, would she? Your mom's got good sense."

"I know, but she gets so tired and it's hard to keep up with the bills and everything."

"But nobody beats her up."

"I know him. He'll swear he's changed."

"She won't fall for that."

Georgia shook her head, but she wasn't so sure.

"If the worst comes to the worst," Angela said, "you can come stay with us."

Georgia was touched. She wanted to say so, but

she didn't quite know how. She got Angela another cup of cocoa. "They wouldn't let me."

"Run away." Angela's face lit up with ideas. "I know a super place where you and Sky could hang out. It's this old deserted farmhouse. It's kind of falling down, but part of it is okay. There's a chimney and an old iron stove. We could get some wood, and you could keep a fire going . . ."

"What would I eat?" She was beginning to catch Angela's enthusiasm.

"I'll sneak you stuff."

"Where would Sky live?"

"Outdoors, silly. Where do you think she's lived all her life?"

It began to sound wonderful. "Where is it?"

"Way up beyond Eight Mile Canyon. I used to go there sometimes when my mother was sick. It's real quiet."

"I could sing at the top of my lungs." She frowned. "How would I get to school?"

Angela thought for a minute. "I know! Don't go!"

Georgia laughed. What a wonderful idea! "I have to get an education though."

"I'll come every day and bring my homework. I'll take good notes and everything. So it'll be just as good as if you'd been there. And the truant officer won't look for you 'cause he'll think you went home with your mother."

For a few minutes Georgia contemplated the

joys of such a life. Then she shook her head. "I'd never get away with it. My mom wouldn't just go off and leave me."

"She couldn't do anything if she didn't know where you were."

"She'd be unhappy though. I don't want to do that to her."

"No." Angela wrinkled her forehead in thought. "But see, she'd find out how unhappy she was making *you*, so she'd change her mind about going back east."

"Kids don't have that much clout."

"Georgia!" Angela was getting impatient. "Think positive!"

That night after she went to bed, Georgia found herself thinking about it. It was a crazy idea, but it was very appealing. She simply could not leave Sky and go back home. All the old horror and fear would begin again, and she couldn't stand it. If she wasn't there, maybe her parents would get along better. Often it had been Georgia that they had fought over. Her grandmother's ideas about raising a child were not at all like her mother's, and what her grandmother said was what her father believed.

But she would miss her mother. Sooner or later you had to leave your mother anyway, but not yet. She fell asleep finally and dreamed she was standing on a floating ice floe that rocked scarily in the midst of very black cold water.

26

THE DAY she had her first lesson, Angela went along with them, and she and Georgia's mother explored the university campus while Georgia was with Mrs. Trent.

Georgia was very nervous, but Mrs. Trent was easy to talk to. She was about forty, tall and thin and humorous. She made Georgia laugh, and after that, things went well.

At the end of the hour she said, "I think we've got something here, Georgia. But if it's going to pay off for you, you're going to have to work."

"I'll work." Georgia said it with such fervor that Mrs. Trent laughed and patted her shoulder.

She found Angela and her mother waiting for her outside the piano-shaped Music Building. They went to the mall and had giros while she told them all about Mrs. Trent. Afterward she and Angela Christmas-shopped. Her biggest purchase was a beautiful dark red horse blanket. Now Sky would be just as classy as any eastern horse. And warm, too.

In a tobacconist's shop she found a tiny pipe for Vera. She got a knitted vest for her mother and a book of Emily Dickinson poetry for Angela, who had been charmed by a poem the teacher had read to them at school, the one that starts "I'm nobody— who are you?" She found a calendar with nice horse pictures for Marty. For quite a while she looked at and rejected gifts for Elmore. Finally she remembered that he liked chocolate-covered cherries, and she bought him a big box. She had grown fond of Elmore, since the day he lifted Marty so gently and took him to the doctor. A father like that you had to love.

She and Angela met Georgia's mother under the big clock, and they bought some Baskin-Robbins to take home. It had been a very good day.

"Wait till you see what I got you for Christmas," she told Sky as soon as they got home. "Angela got you something too, but I won't tell." She gave the horse half an apple and ate the other half herself.

When she went back to the house, her mother was just hanging up the phone. "Georgia," she said. She looked strange, as if she didn't know whether to feel glad or scared.

Before she said it, Georgia knew what she was going to say.

"Your father is flying out for a couple of days."

Georgia backed up against the door. "I won't go."

"Won't go? Where?"

"You know where. He's coming to get us. I won't go."

Her mother shoved her coffeecup across the table. It fell to the floor and broke. "Why don't you listen to me!" Her voice shook. "I didn't say anything about going anywhere. Your father is coming to see us. It's Christmas. That's *all!*"

"It won't be all," Georgia said. She began to pick up the pieces of the broken cup. "It won't be all. You'll see." She flung the pieces into the trash can with a crash. "I'm not going." She ran upstairs to her room.

The next day she asked Angela to take her out to Eight Mile Canyon to see the old farmhouse. They both rode on Sky's back, Angela clinging nervously to Georgia's parka. Georgia kept Sky down to a fast walk, in order not to terrify Angela too much. Anyway, for the last half of the trip the snow was too deep to do more than walk. Sky snorted and tossed her head as if she were enjoying herself. At least one of us will be happy, Georgia thought grimly. The idea of living in a deserted house had lost some of its excitement. Now it was a necessity.

She was dismayed when she saw the place. It was picturesque all right, half standing, half leaning with the roof fallen in.

"Isn't it neat?" Angela said. "Nobody'll ever find you out here."

"I'll freeze to death."

" 'Course you won't. My grandfather used to live out in the woods all winter, without even a shack. He lived under this huge pine tree that must have been a million years old. There was a bank behind the tree that sheltered him. He kept warm all winter."

"I'm not your grandfather." Westerners, she thought, really were a different kind of people. She tried to think of her elegant grandmother living under a tree all winter. It was such a grotesque idea, it almost made her laugh, in spite of the way she was feeling.

Angela was showing off the big fireplace and the wide floor boards, covered now with small animal droppings, pine needles, and dirt.

"I'll need a broom," Georgia said.

"So we'll get a broom. Don't be so negative, Georgia. Look at this neat kitchen stove. It works, too. I've used it."

Georgia wandered into the falling-down part, stepping cautiously over broken flooring. "Sky could stay in here."

"Sure she could. So you've got a house and a stable without even going outdoors."

"There isn't any bathroom," Georgia said.

Angela pointed out the broken window to an outhouse that canted crazily on a small knoll. "You can boil snow for water. We'll get you some of those tablets that purify water. Anyway if you boil it, it's okay."

Georgia began to get back a little of her original

enthusiasm. It would be a challenge, all right. Maybe she could prove that an Easterner could be just as tough as a Westerner. She could do things her grandmother or her father would never be able to do. She'd be a survivor! "I'd need a couple of pots and pans."

"I'll swipe 'em at home. We've got my mother's as well as my sister's. Who needs all that?"

By the time they rode home, Georgia was feeling excited about her adventure. If Angela's grandfather could live under a tree, she could live in a falling-down house by herself. Not really by herself. She'd have Sky, and Angela would come every day. And her radio would work on batteries. Not her stereo though. But someday she'd get one that did.

"Guess what?" She said later to Sky. "You may be going to live practically in the wild."

27

GEORGIA'S MOTHER was worrying. The plane from Boston was arriving at a time when she would be at work.

"Let him take a cab," Georgia said. "Where's he going to stay anyway?" With a sudden alarming thought she said, "Not here, I hope."

"Of course not. I made a reservation at the Sheraton. But it seems awful for nobody to meet him."

Georgia sighed. Now that she had decided she wasn't going back East with them, she worried more on her mother's behalf than on her own. She didn't feel good about the idea of deserting her. Her mother hadn't said she was thinking about going home, but Georgia was sure he would talk her into it. Why else would he come way out here just for three days?

"Do you think Elmore would take you to meet him?" her mother said. She sounded apologetic.

"I don't want to meet him." Then because her mother looked so sad and worried, she said, "All right, I'll ask Elmore."

Her mother kissed her. "It's only for three days."

And then what? Georgia thought.

She went over to the Rosses' and explained the situation. Before she could ask him, Elmore volunteered to go.

"You and me can meet him, sis. No sweat."

But Georgia did sweat, all the way to the airport. For one thing she thought they were going to be late. Her mother would be upset if he got in and there was no one there. He'd have a temper tantrum. Everything would be a mess.

Elmore drove erratically, speeding up and slowing down without visible reason, as if he just got tired of pushing his foot down on the accelerator. The old pickup rattled and squeaked. Georgia would have to sit in the back when her father was there, on old grain sacks and tools. The pickup smelled of sawdust.

Elmore saw her keep glancing at her watch. "Don't worry, sis. It's Johnson-Bell field we're headin' for, not JFK. Won't take us more than five more minutes."

The pickup bounced on the ruts the snow had made. The windshield wipers stuck when Elmore tried to clear the glaze of frost from the glass. "Winter," he said. "You can have it."

Georgia tried to picture her fastidious father sitting where she was sitting now, the heater vent blasting hot air into his face and stirring up the dust on the floor, the empty oil can that bounced under one's feet, the torn upholstery half covered by an imitation sheepskin. Find out how the other half lives, Dad.

She grabbed the door when Elmore made a sharp left turn off the highway into the airport road. In a field sat several old biplanes, and beyond them, on a landing field, there were Piper Cubs and other small prop planes looking like toys.

"Smoke jumpers fly out of here in the summer," Elmore said. "Used to be a smoke jumper myself when I was a whole lot younger."

Georgia looked at him in a new light, trying to picture him as a smoke jumper. "I didn't know that."

"Yep. Wasn't always old and decrepit." He grinned at her. "I was a mechanic in the Air Force too, in the Korean police action. We don't call it a war, you know. But don't let 'em kid you, it was a war."

He parked the pickup in a No Parking zone. They walked into the low airport building.

"Hey, Pete, how you doin'?" Elmore said to a security man. And to Georgia he said, "Right on the nose," as a big Northwest jet circled and came in low. "You gotta know your stuff to land on this field. You miss and you want to lift up, and what have you got right in your face? Mountains."

They went upstairs to meet the incoming passengers. Georgia's stomach was tight. She really didn't know how to behave with her father. It was such a weird situation. She didn't know how he would act with her either. She wished with all her might that he wouldn't get off the plane, that he might have missed it or something.

At first she thought she was getting her wish. A stream of passengers filed into the waiting room, getting hugged by their people, or rushing by as if they had to meet somebody somewhere else, but there was no sign of her father. One of the flight attendants stood in the doorway of the plane with her hat and coat on and her suitcase with its little wheels beside her.

Then her father strolled off, wearing his four-year-old Brooks Brothers coat that Grandmother had given him and managing to look neat and well-dressed in spite of a flight nearly all the way across the country. She tried to smile as she stepped forward to meet him. He was wearing the fur-lined gloves she had given him three Christmases ago.

He smiled at her the same way he always did, as if she were someone he knew slightly. "Hello, Georgia. How are you? Good to see you." He gave her a brief hug. He smelled of cigarette smoke and Faberge Brut, just as always.

"Mom had to work. She'll come to the hotel later." She introduced him to Elmore.

He glanced at him and said, "How are you."

"Did you eat on the plane?" Georgia asked him.

He made a face. "Horrible stuff."

"Well, Mom's going to take you to dinner. She asked to get off early, about eight, if that's okay with you." And if it isn't, tough luck, she thought.

There was an awkward pause. Elmore filled it. "Well, sir, you got some baggage?"

"A black pigskin suitcase, small, and a two-suiter. They've got bright blue tags on them. You can't miss them."

Quietly Elmore said, "I'll get 'em. Meet you by the doors, Georgia." He headed for the stairs.

Georgia was angry. Her father was treating Elmore like a porter or something. "Daddy, Elmore is a friend of ours. It was nice of him to take the time to come meet you."

"Sure, fine," he said. "I appreciate it."

But she knew he didn't. She looked at Elmore disappearing into the stairwell and saw him as her father did: a short, broad man with huge shoulders and arms, his faded work overalls, his clean worn denim shirt, the old sheepskin vest, the shapeless black hat squarely on the middle of his head. Her father would never see the kindness in the pale blue eyes, the touch of humor in the mouth that was nearly covered by an untidy handlebar moustache, the strength that had lifted his son, the caring. She felt like running after Elmore and saying, "Forgive my father."

She prayed that her father wouldn't show his surprise at the old pickup. He was, she realized, a terrible snob. She had never thought about that before. Maybe it hadn't come up. Of course, she'd always known that Grandmother was a snob. Grandmother even looked down on Mom because Mom came from a poor family and worked her way through college waiting on tables. Just like she's doing now. It wasn't fair.

It was hard to make conversation with her father, feeling as angry as she did. Yes, Dad, school is fine. Yes, Dad, I like Montana a lot. Yes, I have a horse of my own. No, nothing fancy, just a mustang.

She was saved from having to explain what a mustang was by Elmore's arrival with the bag and the two-suiter. Her father took the two-suiter and left Elmore to carry the bag. Well, Mom used to say, when she got mad, that he was brought up to think he was the crown prince.

She sat in the back on a gunny sack and endured her father's glance of amusement. She could see him thinking that the west was just as barbaric as he had expected it to be. Her own temper seethed.

Elmore was speaking about the weather, and her father was making absentminded replies, trying to see out through the iced-over window. Elmore pulled up in the circular drive at the entrance to the Sheraton, got out and took her father's luggage inside. Georgia stayed where she was.

"You aren't coming in?" her father said.

"I have to get home. I have things to do. Mom will be here in about an hour and a half."

He tightened his mouth in the way that meant he was displeased. "I've come a long way, Georgia."

"You must be tired," she said, deliberately misunderstanding him.

He gave her a long look and then got out. "Good night, then."

"Good night." She watched him walk into the hotel with his quick, almost arrogant walk. The big banker. The big banker who had such a lousy disposition he couldn't hold a job.

When Elmore came back to the pickup, she got in front.

"I hope he thanked you," she said.

Elmore scratched his moustache. "Wasn't necessary."

She ground her teeth. "Well, I thank you, and Mom thanks you. I'm sorry. I'm sorry he's so—"

Gently he cut her off. "Hold on, sis, hold on there. Don't say nothing you'll be sorry for. You and me understand each other. Nothin' to worry about." He smiled his warm, gap-toothed smile.

She stared out the window, her eyes full of tears.

28

"HE'S LOOKING GOOD, isn't he," Georgia's mother said at breakfast. "His new job seems to agree with him."

Georgia put down her fork with a small clatter. "Are you going back?"

Her mother looked startled. "Oh, I don't think so, Georgia. I'm not ready for that."

But you will be, Georgia said to herself. He'll talk you into it. He can be very persuasive. He'll tell you how he's conquered his temper and everything's going to be dandy. She pushed her plate aside and got up from the table.

"Georgia . . . ?"

But she had already grabbed her coat and her bookbag and was going out the door.

"How'd it go?" Angela said to her at recess.

Georgia shrugged. "Same old Dad. And Mom's

saying how good he looks . . ." She bit her lip. All morning she had been fighting against tears.

"Listen," Angela said, "I know a lot of dirty tricks. If he comes out to your house, I could play some of them on him."

"Like what?"

"Oh, letting the air out of his tires . . ."

"He hasn't got a car."

"Well, I'll think of something."

Georgia shook her head. "I just hope Mom doesn't go back till spring, so it would be a little warmer in my deserted house."

"You really think she'll go?"

"I can tell she's softening up. He'll behave himself and make promises, and she'll fall for it. After all, she married the guy."

"Well, if she hadn't, I wouldn't have known you."

Georgia smiled. Angela was a good friend. "I just hope he doesn't make fun of Sky. If he does, I'll explode. I couldn't *stand* that."

"Keep Sky in the barn. It's only a couple of days."

He was there when Georgia got home from school. It was her mother's night off, and she was cooking up a storm. He was lolling on the sofa with his feet on the old leather hassock as if he owned the place. Both of them looked as if they were feeling fine. Georgia's heart sank. There wasn't a hope.

"Come over here and tell me all about your life,"

he said to Georgia, patting the sofa beside him. When he did get friendly with her, he talked as if she were still six or seven years old.

She started to make an excuse, but her mother gave her an imploring look, so she sat down on the edge of the sofa, as far away from him as she could. "My life's fine."

He glanced around the room with amusement. "You like this palace, do you?"

"I like it fine."

"Well, kids will adapt to anything, I guess. What are you learning in school?"

She shrugged. "The same things you learn in any school, I guess."

He and her mother exchanged glances.

"Don't be rude, honey," her mother said. "Your dad is interested."

"Well, what can I say? We have English and history and algebra and general science, just like at home."

As soon as she could, she excused herself and went out to the barn to feed Sky. "I can't stand it," she told her horse. "He acts so snide about everything. As if everything *he* has is perfect. I like it here. I just hope he doesn't come out to see you. Maybe he's forgotten about you." She leaned against the horse. "Just remember, I'll never leave you. We'll go to the old house and have a happy life together. Angela will come see us every day, and after they stop looking for me, we'll visit with the Rosses."

At dinner he asked about her music lessons and

then didn't really listen while she told him. He was so busy playing up to her mom, he hardly knew she existed.

She excused herself to do homework as soon as she had finished with the dishes. "Twenty-four hours from now," she told the kittens, "he'll be gone." She removed Pang from the back of her neck. "You guys can live in the old house with Sky and me. We'll have a ball." Tears squeezed out of her eyes in spite of her effort not to let them. "We'll live free the way Sky used to, and we'll all be very, very happy." She buried her face in her pillow.

29

WHAT SHE HAD DREADED had happened: he had spent the night. They were still in bed when she came downstairs to get her breakfast. It wasn't unusual for her to eat breakfast alone; her mother often slept in when she had worked late. But this time Georgia resented it bitterly. A mother was supposed to get her kid's breakfast, wasn't she? It would serve her right if Georgia didn't eat any breakfast at all and got anorexia or something.

She slammed her cereal bowl onto the table. If they were spending the night together, the fight was all over. Sure as sure, her mother would tell her tonight that they were going back.

Well, I've got news for you, Mother. You're going alone. Only she couldn't tell her that. It had to be a secret. A couple of hours before her mother was ready to go, Georgia would just take off with her horse and her kittens. And never be found again. Except when she wanted to be.

She pushed her cereal away half eaten and gave the kittens some food. They were getting to be big. Teenagers, she told them, like me.

She ran out to the barn a few minutes before the bus came, to say good morning and have a nice day to Sky. The little horse was restless.

"I know, you're sick of staying inside. As soon as he goes, I'll take you for a good long ride, I promise. Try not to get anxious while I'm gone. Dream about our house." She kissed Sky's nose and ran as she heard the bus.

She hoped he would be gone by the time she got home, but her mother's car was still there. She must have made arrangements at the restaurant so she could take him to the airport. What if she had already quit her job? The thought hit Georgia like a knife. So soon?

When she came into the house, they were both there, and his bags were packed. She looked quickly at her mother. She was smiling. Bad sign.

"Georgia," he said, smiling his flashy smile, "I haven't seen your horse."

"Oh, she's just a horse," Georgia said quickly.

"I want to see her. Let's go down to the barn and have a look."

"It's not much of a horse, I'm afraid," her mother said.

Georgia felt betrayed.

"So we'll take a look." He hooked his arm through her mother's and put his free hand on Georgia's shoulder.

She moved away from him and grimly led the way to the barn. If he made fun of Sky . . .

"Not exactly the Meadowbrook Stables, is it," he said, looking at the barn as they went in.

"It's mine," Georgia said. "And the Meadowbrook Stables isn't."

"Aren't," he said. "Are you sure you're getting A's in English?"

"She's getting A's in everything." Her mother sounded a little nervous.

Georgia leaned against the stall. "So there she is."

He blinked in the dim light and came closer. Sky turned her head to see who was there. She stomped her foot and whinnied. He stared at her as if he couldn't believe his eyes. Then he laughed.

"My God," he said, "this is pitiful. A kid of mine riding a brokendown scarecrow like this? Amy, how could you let her?"

"I didn't exactly have the money for a thoroughbred," Georgia's mother said sharply. "She loves the horse. Leave her alone."

"Are you kidding? After all the money I spent on that kid's riding lessons, I should let her choose a runt like this? Get rid of her, Georgia. To the glue factory or wherever. I'll buy you a decent horse when you get home."

Georgia's voice was so choked, she could hardly speak. "I'm not going home."

"Don't be silly." He gave Sky a contemptuous slap on the rump.

Instantly Sky's hooves flashed out and crashed against the stall door. There was a sound of splintering wood. Her father jumped back, his face mottled with anger. He looked around and saw an old whip hanging high on the wall, where the previous tenants had left it. He grabbed it and came toward Sky.

"Don't you touch her!"

He paid no attention to Georgia. She dived at him and began kicking him in the shins. He swore and pushed her off and she felt the sting of the whip around her legs.

"Put that whip down!" Georgia's mother grabbed the pitchfork and aimed it at him.

For a minute he stared at her as if he couldn't believe his eyes.

"I mean it, drop the whip."

"You wouldn't have the nerve . . ."

"Oh yes, I would. Yes, I would." She waited until, very slowly, he let the whip fall to the floor. "Go get in the car, Bob."

Sky was stomping and jerking her head.

"In the car," Georgia's mother said. "I'll take you to the airport. And that's the end."

"You promised . . ."

"I promised nothing. I said I'd see. Well, I see."

Georgia said, "Do you want me to come with you?"

"No. Stay here and quiet Sky. I'll be all right."

"But what if he . . ."

"He won't. I have my CB. And the police here are my friends."

Georgia's father looked at her, and she saw the glare in his eyes. He's sick, she thought. It was the first time it had occurred to her. It's a sickness. She felt her hatred melt into something like pity.

30

THE SCHOOL CONCERT took place three days before Christmas. It was perfect Christmas weather, clear and cold with about two inches of fresh snow.

At a suggestion from the music teacher, Georgia sang "Silent Night" in both German and English, and for an encore she sang "Greensleeves." Angela stood in the wings wringing her hands with nervousness. Georgia's mother and the Rosses were in the front row.

"Well, I didn't exactly bring the house down, and there was no standing ovation," she said to Angela afterward.

"You got as much applause as anybody. I timed 'em. You should have had a lot more. But what do they know." Angela's eyes were shiny. "I thought you were a star."

Georgia hugged her, and both of them looked

surprised. "I wouldn't have done it at all if you hadn't talked me into it."

After the concert was over, they all went into Missoula, and Elmore treated everybody to crepes at the Apple Tree. Looking around at the faces of her friends, Georgia thought it was the happiest Christmas she had ever had. And in a couple of days she would give Sky her present, the beautiful new blanket. The one Marty had let her use was motheaten and worn. Sky deserved the best blanket in existence.

ON CHRISTMAS DAY Angela and her little brother Stevie came to Georgia's house for the Christmas tree. Georgia had bought a little fringed suede vest for Stevie. "Like cowboys wear," she told him. He put it on and galloped around the room on his imaginary stallion. Then they all went to the Rosses' later for a goose dinner.

Georgia had kept Sky in the barn for two days because there had been a high, bitterly cold wind; but on the day after Christmas, the sun came out and the wind died down. The world looked so sparkling, it dazzled the eyes. Georgia and Angela and Stevie, who had come along with her again, went out to the barn to let Sky out into the pasture. She nickered impatiently when she saw them. She was wearing her new blanket.

"Can I ride her?" Stevie's eyes were big with admiration.

Georgia hesitated. She knew how much he longed to get on the horse's back, and she wanted to let him; but Sky had been shut up for a while, and she was feeling skittish. "Let's let her run off some of that steam first," she said. "Then you can."

"Okay. I like her tail. It's real black."

Angela sneezed. "Sky is beautiful."

Georgia led the horse out to the pasture and turned her loose. The three of them leaned on the fence watching her race up and down, her black mane lifting in the breeze that she created.

"She hates to be shut up," Georgia said. "But it was so cold." Marty would laugh if he heard her. And he was right. Sky was used to any kind of weather; but that didn't mean she had to like it.

Sky showed no signs of slowing down.

"When can I ride her?" Stevie said.

"Take it easy, Steve," Angela said. "She needs to stretch her legs."

"I need to stretch my legs."

Angela laughed. "Run around then."

As Stevie galloped up and down on his black stallion Charlie, Angela said, "So you won't be moving into the old farmhouse after all."

"No. Everything's okay now." She was thoughtful for a second. "I feel sorry for my father. He's really got a head problem. I never realized that before."

"He ought to see a shrink."

"He never will though. And my grandmother will keep telling him he's fine."

"Your mom seems more relaxed."

"Yes, she does." It always surprised Georgia that Angela noticed so much. "I guess because she finally made up her mind."

Sky began to slow down some.

"Now?" Stevie said.

"I'll go talk to her." Georgia slid off the fence and started across the pasture toward Sky. The horse came to a stop and looked at Georgia as if she were trying to figure out what she was going to do.

As Georgia got closer, she held out her hand. Sky threw up her head, wheeled, and began to gallop the length of the pasture, toward the west end.

"Oh, come on," Georgia said. "Cut it out. I've got a carrot. Later we can go for a ride up to the mountain . . ."

But Sky had picked up speed, and when she came to the fence, she gathered herself together and sailed over it with inches to spare.

"Oh, no! Sky!" Georgia began to run.

She climbed over the fence, awkward in her haste, and took off after Sky, calling as she ran. Sky never slackened speed. She galloped along the outside of the Rosses' fence, her hooves pounding the earth.

Frightened, Georgia stood still. Sky was heading for the chain link fence with its barbed wire top, where the black Angus clustered at the far end of that pasture. In a strangled voice, Georgia called, "Sky! No!"

With the eight inches of barbed wire, the fence stood higher than either Georgia's or the Rosses.' But Sky jumped without hesitation. Her left hind hoof caught in the barbed wire. The momentum of her leap tore the hoof loose. She screamed and fell sprawling on her side.

She was struggling to get up as Georgia reached the fence. The farmer who owned the place came running from the barnyard and opened the gate for her.

"Bad spill," he said.

Angela came running, with Stevie trailing a long way behind her. "Is she hurt bad?"

Sky was trembling violently, blood streaming from the injured hoof. Gently and efficiently the farmer examined the hoof.

"Raked her through the hoof and up the pastern. You'll need Doc Fessenden. I'll call him. You stay with her. You all right yourself?"

Georgia felt as if she were going to faint, but she said, "I'm okay."

"I'll stay with her," Angela said.

Georgia held Sky's head, stroking her and murmuring to her. "The vet will fix it. Don't be scared. You'll be as right as rain in a few days. Remember how Marty got his leg hurt, and now he's okay? These things happen."

"If Stevie hadn't wanted to ride her," Angela began.

"No, don't. It just happened."

Sky looked around, the whites of her eyes showing, as if the danger was outside herself. She held her hoof off the ground and trembled.

It seemed years before the farmer came back. "He's on his way. Fess is a good man." He looked at the hoof again and shook his head.

"What is it?" Georgia said. "Is it bad?"

"Sometimes hard to heal when they cut into the hoof like that."

"Sky will heal," she said. "Sky's very strong and healthy."

He looked at her sympathetically. "You the new people down the road?"

She nodded.

"One of Marty's little mustangs, is she?"

"Yes."

"I'll give him a ring on the horn. We maybe could use his help."

"Thanks." When he had gone, she put her arms around Sky's neck. "It'll be all right, I know it will. Some people are just gloomy. Don't step on it, though." She stroked Sky's nose, but Sky turned her head away. Stevie caught up with them and stood silently.

It seemed years before she heard the vet's car and Marty arriving almost at the same time. Marty gave Sky a searching look and shot a look at Georgia. Then he stood at Sky's head to steady her while the vet examined the hoof. The bleeding had stopped. Sky quivered and shied as the vet touched her, but he was gentle and quick. He got some medication from his bag and painted the wound. Georgia thought of the day Sky got leaves stuck all over her feet, and tears stung her eyes. They should have left her in her mountains. Maybe nothing would have happened to her. But she knew that didn't make sense. All kinds of bad things could have happened.

Dr. Fessenden was binding up the pastern. "Either of you guys got a horse trailer? I'd like to move her over to her own place, put her in the stable for a while. You got a stall for her, Miss?"

"Yes. She's got a stall."

"I got a horse trailer," the farmer said. "Hold on a couple minutes, and I'll back her down here."

While they waited, the vet gave Sky a shot. The horse tried to jump sideways as she felt the needle, but on three feet she was clumsy and nearly fell.

"That's all right, girl, that's all right now." Dr. Fessenden was soothing her. "That'll make it feel better." He gave Georgia an envelope with some huge capsules. "If you can get one of these into her every four or five hours, that'll keep her quieted down." He looked at Marty. "Maybe you'd give her a hand."

"Sure. Sure I will." Marty looked upset. "Georgia, why don't you go along home and get the stall ready. Get her some fresh water and a blanket and some pellets. I'll be along after a while."

Georgia didn't want to leave Sky, but Marty said, "Take her home, Angela."

Georgia went. She couldn't bear to see them loading Sky into the trailer. It would frighten her even if it didn't hurt her. She had to trust Marty.

Angela and Stevie went with her, and then while Angela took Stevie home, Georgia swept out the stall and filled a bucket with fresh water. Sky would be all right. She had to be all right. The new blanket would keep her warm and comfortable. But Sky would hate having to stand around in the barn while her hoof healed. Georgia would have to spend a lot of time with her. At night she'd leave her transistor radio turned on, so Sky would have something to listen to. There was that new twenty-four-hour station that played music all the time.

Angela came back. She looked pale, and she didn't have much to say. She got the broom and swept out the whole barn, as if she couldn't stand it not to be doing something. Georgia was thankful for Angela's friendship. It helped.

They stood back when the truck and trailer came into the yard. Dr. Fessenden came right behind them. The men had trouble getting Sky out of the trailer. Georgia could hardly stand it. She felt helpless.

If only there were something she could do so Sky wouldn't feel so scared. It was terrible for a horse to lose the use of a foot. Their feet were their safety, the way a bird's wings were.

At last they had her in the stall. In a few minutes

Dr. Fessenden came out and looked at Georgia. His expression frightened her.

"Tough little horse," he said.

"She's real healthy."

"The only thing is . . ." He frowned. "When they cut up a hoof like that, it doesn't usually heal."

She felt as if he had hit her in the chest. "*Ever?*"

"I don't like to say ever, but I have to say I never saw one that did."

The farmer joined them. "It's a real shame. Never would have put up that barbed wire if I thought a horse would try to jump it. I got rid of my horses a couple years ago. Just got cattle now."

"It wasn't your fault," Georgia said in a low voice. "She ran away. She jumped our fence."

"Real good jumper. Only I guess she won't be jumping no more."

Marty gave him a hard look, and then said, "Thanks for the use of the trailer, Harry. Need any help?"

The man took the hint. "No, no. That's all right. Glad I could help." He looked at Georgia as if he wanted to say something, but then he shook his head and went away.

"I'll stop by tomorrow," Dr. Fessenden said. "I'm sorry, Georgia."

She and Marty and Angela were left alone with Sky. The horse was quiet now, drooping a little, standing on her three good legs.

"That shot he gave her, that'll help," Marty said.

"I'll come back after supper, and we'll give her the capsule. That'll keep her quiet during the night. Doc Fessenden's a good man."

"Marty," Georgia said.

"Yeah?" He avoided looking at her, fussing with a bridle that hung on a nail.

"What's going to happen to her?"

He looked at her. "You want it straight?"

"Please."

"Well . . ." He hesitated for a long moment. "It don't look like she's going to get to use that foot again."

"Ever?"

"Don't look like it."

"She can't just stand around on three feet. She'd go crazy."

"No, she can't live that way."

"So what happens?" Her hands were clenched so tight, she could feel the nails cutting into her palms.

He looked away. "She'll have to be shot." He looked at her with anguish in his eyes. "I'd rather be shot myself than tell you . . ."

"I know," she said. "I know. Thanks." She ran to the house and sat on the edge of her bed and rocked back and forth. There were no tears. Angela stood in the doorway watching her, silent, with tears streaking her own face.

31

"THE VET will be here in a few minutes," Georgia said, the next afternoon.

"I think Sky looks better." Angela was stroking the horse's nose.

"You aren't sneezing."

"I think I outgrew it."

Sky hung her head as if she felt depressed. Uneasily she moved on her three healthy hooves, now and then touching the wounded one to the floor of the stall and pulling it up again quickly.

"Some wounds take a long time to heal," Georgia said.

"I know it. My mother had a compound fracture of her elbow one time and it took forever." She broke off as if realizing that she was not offering the best example. "But she got over it. I was five. I couldn't understand why she had that thing on her arm and the sling and all. She couldn't pick me up."

Georgia jumped at the sound of a car coming in the yard. "It's the vet."

Dr. Fessenden came in carrying his black bag. He went into the stall, talked to Sky a minute, and then hunkered down to look at the hoof.

It seemed to Georgia that it took him a very long time. When he straightened up, he sighed and patted Sky's back. Sky turned her head to look at him. Then she looked at Georgia. Her eyes had lost their bright, alert look.

Dr. Fessenden came out of the stall and put his arm around Georgia's shoulders. Angela gave him a searching look and then went outside. "Georgia," he said, "I hate to tell you this, but that little horse isn't going to get any better."

"Yes, she is." Georgia said it fast to keep him from going on. "It just takes time."

He looked away. "This is what I don't like about being a vet. The ones you lose. I'm so sorry."

Georgia swallowed hard. "You mean she's going to die? From a cut on the foot?"

"No, I mean you're going to have to put her down. It's cruel, letting her just stand there and fall apart. That's not any life for a proud little horse, a wild horse at that. Look at her."

Georgia looked at Sky and quickly looked away.

"That wire went right through to the frog, right

[*177*]

in the sole of her foot. It's horny, elastic stuff, and there's no way it's going to mend. You've got to have her shot, honey."

"No!" She grabbed the rough wood of the stall side with both hands. A splinter of wood jabbed into her finger. It hurt, and she was glad of it.

"I can do it for you, but Marty said he'd like to take care of things if it came to that. Guess he knew it would. Marty's a good man with horses. Georgia, she won't know what hit her. She'll go out while she's still . . ."

Georgia cried, "No, no, no!" and ran out of the stable. In the pasture, she ran and ran the length of it and back again, until finally she fell onto the snow and sobbed.

When she sat up at last, Angela was sitting beside her, her own face streaked with tears.

Georgia wiped her face with a Kleenex and stood up. "I've got to go talk to Marty."

32

GEORGIA TRIED to keep her voice steady as she talked to her mother. "Marty says he can . . . shoot her, or if I want to sell her to the canner, they'll pay me three hundred and fifty dollars. You could use the money. You need to get the car fixed."

"Georgia . . ." Her mother leaned toward her. "You do what's least painful for you. Never mind about the money. Sure we could use it, but I think I can get a small loan from the bank to get the car fixed."

"You always said don't borrow money."

"Sometimes it's necessary."

"It wouldn't be if I . . ." She pulled a slip of paper from her shirt pocket. "This is the number of the cannery. Will you call them? I don't know if I could. It's a long distance number, Spokane."

"Georgia, are you sure you want to do this?"

Georgia clamped her mouth tight for a moment.

"Yes. They'll ask you if she's able to stand up in the truck for the drive to Spokane. They won't take her if she isn't. You tell them yes, she is." She left the room quickly.

A little later her mother found her in her room and said, "They'll come probably in three or four days. They have to wait till there are enough horses—" She broke off. "Oh, honey, I am so sorry."

Georgia nodded. She had her radio tuned to the university station. They were playing *Rigoletto*. She lay rigid on the bed, trying to pay attention. It was the duet scene in Act One, Scene Two, with Rigoletto and the Assassin. She got up suddenly, shut it off, got her parka, and went outside. She didn't look toward the stable.

To the mountains, that's where she wanted to go; toward Eight Mile Canyon and Woodchuck Mountain, where she and Sky had ridden. Then she hadn't known the names of those places. Vera was right, a person ought to know things by their real names.

It was best not to think of Sky. She thought about her voice lessons instead. They were going well. The teacher said they'd have a lot of work to do together. Well, of course they'd have work to do. That was why you took lessons.

What if Dr. Fessenden was wrong?

She wished she had gotten a wreath to hang on Sky's door for Christmas. Sky would have liked that. She'd thought of it and then not done it. There had been the blanket though. Sky could wear that when she went away.

What if Dr. Fessenden was mistaken?

She turned back, and when she got to her own place, she was almost running. There was some sugar in her pocket for Sky. She ran into the barn thinking maybe there would have been a big change. Maybe Sky would be looking like herself again.

But she wasn't. She seemed thin, and her coat was dull. Her eyes had no more mischief in them. Georgia put her arm around the horse's neck. "Jesus was born in a stable, maybe sort of like this one," she said. "That's how you got the blanket, to celebrate his birthday. Things didn't turn out too great for him, but he went to heaven. Nobody can tell me horses don't go to heaven, too. And there are probably mountains for you to run in. Heaven is kind of confusing to think about, but maybe what the best part of you loves, you get. So I'll get you."

After a while she went into the house. Angela had given her a present and she had loved it when she opened it. It was even more important now.

She held it in her hands and felt as if the world had stopped. It was an enlarged framed picture that Angela had taken of Sky about a month ago. It was a side view, with Sky's head turned toward the camera with her old look of curiosity and mischief. For a long time Georgia sat looking at it. It was the best present she had ever had.

33

GEORGIA TRIED not to watch for the truck, but every time she heard a car coming down the road, she went to look. Angela came over and tried to get her to go cross-country skiing. She even offered to let Georgia use her new skis and she would use her old home-made ones; but Georgia didn't want to leave the place, just in case.

When Angela left, she went to the stable and hung on the half-door talking to Sky. "I dreamed last night that you were Pegasus, you turned into Sky-Pegasus, and I rode you across the sky. It was wonderful. I could feel the wind, soft and warm. Your mane lifted in the wind and you galloped on air." She leaned her forehead against Sky's head. "Mom says she learned in college that energy is never lost. If anybody is made of energy, you are. Not maybe so much right now because you don't feel good, but Sky, you were pure energy." She smiled, remembering. "You were such a tough little horse."

She stiffened. The sound of a truck. For a minute she stood perfectly still. Then she gave Sky one long despairing look and ran out into the yard.

The big truck had three horses in it. They looked thin and sick. There were two men in the cab. One of them jumped down and said cheerily, "Hi. You got a horse for us?"

She nodded, unable to speak.

He whipped out a clipboard and a ballpoint pen, and the other man climbed down. "You own the horse?" the first one said. "Sign here." He pointed with a grimy finger.

She signed her name in an unfamiliar scrawl.

"In the stable?"

She nodded, and they started toward the stable. She heard her mother call her. "Marty," she said, as she ran past the porch. "I've got to get Marty."

Marty would stop them. She'd tell him to. He'd explain to them. She'd pay them for their time, because they had come here to get Sky, and she couldn't let Sky go.

She pounded up onto the Ross porch, knocked, and went in. Vera looked startled. She was stirring something on the stove.

"What's the matter?"

"Where's Marty? The men are here to take Sky. I want him to stop them . . ."

Vera put down her spoon and took hold of Georgia's shoulders. "Easy, honey, easy now. She's got to go, you know that. You don't want Marty to have to shoot her."

"Where is he?"

"He went into town to do some errands. Georgia, honey, take it easy." She put her arms around her.

Georgia was breathing so hard, she thought she was going to choke. "I can't," she said with her face against Vera's breast. "I can't."

"It'll be all right. They don't hurt them. Marty looked into it . . ."

"They'll kill her. She'll turn into . . . into dog food . . ."

"Baby, we all turn into some kind of food. That's what keeps life going. Me, I'll nourish the earth. You might turn into a bunch of wild flowers. Life goes round and round."

Georgia got her breathing under control and freed herself from Vera's arms. "All right. Thanks, Vera. Tell Marty when he comes. I better go back."

"That's my brave girl."

Georgia walked slowly along the road. She saw the truck pull out of the yard and drive the other way. What if Dr. Fessenden was wrong? She should have seen another vet. What if he was wrong? "Wait!" She began to run after the truck. But though she ran and ran, the distance between them lengthened. Her chest hurt from running, and she got a pain in her side.

A pickup coming toward her stopped suddenly, skidding a little in the gravel. Marty jumped out and grabbed her. "I saw them," he said. "I know."

She clung to him, crying.

"I know, kid, I know." His arms were tight around her. "It'll be all right, kid. Later when you feel like it, you can have any horse I got. Don't cry, George. It'll be all right."

34

SHE AND ANGELA sat on Angela's front steps. Georgia had been invited to lunch on the last day of Christmas vacation. It was a sunny day and the snow on the ground sparkled like tiny diamonds. Young Stevie was lying on his stomach on his new sled, pushing it along with his feet.

"Where's Charlie?" Georgia said to him.

"Who's Charlie?"

"Your horse. Remember? Your black stallion."

"Oh yeah. I put him away for the winter."

"That was smart."

"He'd get his feet wet in the snow."

There was a knocking sound over their heads.

"There's that crazy woodpecker," Angela said. "It's a wonder we got a house left."

Georgia looked up. She was always surprised at how big these western woodpeckers were. This one was perched on the side of the house, his tail spread against the windowpane for support. He was speckled gray, with a black velvet vest and two bright red circles on his cheeks like a clown. He flew down to the railing of the porch and peered at them, his very long thin beak slightly turned up. His eyes were bright.

"They're sassy birds," Angela said. "Look at that beak, like Bob Hope's nose. Ski-jump."

Georgia looked at the bird. He reminded her of Sky. That same perkiness and alertness. Maybe she'd always be finding Sky all over the place, if she looked. It was a comfort to think so. And though there never would be another horse like Sky, maybe some day there would be one almost as good. It seemed impossible...and yet...they were here in Montana to stay. And in Montana there were lots of horses.